Love & BUBBLES

Edited by
Jaylee James
and
Jennifer Lee Rossman

Love & Bubbles

Copyright © 2018 by Jaylee James

Copyright of individual stories belongs to the author credited.

Cover by: Kyra Wolff - kyrajwolff.com

ISBN: 9781728944425

www.jayleejames.com

Email: jaylee@jayleejames.com

Printed in the U.S.A.

TABLE OF CONTENTS

Trigger and content warnings are displayed beneath each title.

SUMMONED

by Minerva Cerridwen

"...And to finish this morning's Shell News, we want to warn you that humans will be filming below the ocean surface until Thursday. If you want to be certain of your privacy, better stay indoors or check the schedules on..."

Percival moved the large conch shell away from his ear and listened intently. Yes, that was definitely the clatter of his neighbor's mailbox.

With some difficulty, the elderly merman hoisted himself out of his comfortable armchair, dumped the still-talking Resonator Radio shell on the seat, and swam out the door. Rhumba, his gray catfish, quit hovering over the living room carpet in search of crumbs and followed him curiously.

Not that it was a great mystery what Percival was up to. He would be there practically every morning when his neighbor was home. Some days he'd just float in the doorway and admire Larimar: a horned demon, slightly shorter than Percival, with eyes like the void, thirteen tentacles starting below the waist, and light-blue scales that reflected every ray of light in all the colors of the rainbow. On other days, Percival would feel brave enough to approach Larimar for a chat.

Today he was going to be particularly bold. Finally, for the first time in the year the demon had lived here, he was going to

5

ask them over for a cup of tea.

At least, that was the theory. It wasn't exactly the first time he'd resolved to do this.

"Good morning!" Crossing the small front yard to the stone mansion with the crow-stepped gable and the coral windows, Percival attempted to square his shoulders, but he knew there was no way of making his back look less hunched.

"Hello, Percival." Larimar's voice was smooth, almost fluid. "Please keep Rhumba away from my roses, okay?"

"Of course." Percival glared at the fish, as if that had ever impressed it. If only his entire skeleton wouldn't protest at the mere thought of bending down to scoop the pet into his arms... "You're wearing a new... thing." He gestured at the black pendant around Larimar's neck, hoping to distract them from Rhumba's inclination to misbehave.

"It's sea glass," Larimar said, touching it. "I collect them on my days off."

"Ah. Not a gift from one of your employers, then," Percival said, before realizing he might have sounded more disapproving than intended. "Have you received any more of that spinach?" he asked quickly.

"No. I haven't been to land in a while."

As if Percival hadn't noticed. The days when Larimar was away for work were dreary and uneventful. After his husband passed away, Percival had lived as a hermit for nearly a decade. He didn't have any friends, and aside from his monologues to the seaweed in his backyard, these small morning chats were his only chance at social interaction. When the demon was summoned away for several days and occasionally even weeks, it didn't exactly do wonders for Percival's mood. However, the spinach Larimar sometimes brought back was almost worth it.

"Well..." Clearly bored with Percival's silence, Larimar

6

twisted together some of their tentacles.

Percival had to say something. He didn't want to spend the entire day regretting yet another wasted opportunity. But he'd sound like a clownfish if he asked Larimar whether they liked cookies, because who didn't like cookies?

Luring them into his house with the promise that the shells were very interesting today wasn't any use either. Larimar could just listen to their own shells. Besides, calling them interesting would be a gross exaggeration. Larimar would be bored before they were even inside.

On the other hand, Percival couldn't just ask if Larimar felt like having a cup of tea without any kind of smooth bridge, could he? Not when Larimar was bound to own a better brand of tea, won from one of those hateful people who called them away all the time. What if they laughed in Percival's face at the very offer?

"Good day, then." Larimar's forked tail swished through the water and almost tangled with their tentacles as they turned around.

"Larimar, wait!" Percival had to risk it. He couldn't go through another empty, lonely day. Even rejection would be better than that. He all but did a somersault as he burst forward, steadying himself with a hand on the demon's right flipper.

Larimar stared at him in shock.

"I... I'm sorry." Percival immediately tried to pull back his hand, but he couldn't. It was as though his skin were glued fast to Larimar's. "What..."

Everything went dark. They were sucked into a swirl of dark blue, and then smacked down on a hard surface.

Percival blinked and groaned. Everything was too white and too bright. The air was awfully dry, and cold – his shivers made every joint protest.

"Oh!" a loud, high voice called. "Did you bring company,

7

Larry?"

"Don't. Call. Me. Larry." Larimar didn't sound like their melodic self at all. Instead, it was as if they were talking around a mouth full of seaweed, every consonant moist and gurgling.

Percival would have felt amused if he hadn't been in so much pain.

"You do realize this isn't exactly work fit for a demon." Larimar stood upright on their thirteen tentacles and glared at the human female who'd summoned them. The blue pentagram on the living room's tile floor stood out against the neutral tones of her interior, as did her own yellow raincoat.

"Oh, don't be so grumpy," Anemone said, smiling. "You know I always pay up. What do you want this time? Let me guess, spinach again?"

Larimar ignored her and crouched next to Percival, who was still lying down in the middle of the pentagram, pale green hair fanned out around his midnight blue head. "Hey, are you okay? You... You can breathe here, right?"

"Of course I can breathe. I spent half my youth on beaches," Percival snapped, slowly sitting upright. In spite of the lack of water, his voice was surprisingly clear. "What is this place? Why are we here?"

"I was summoned," Larimar muttered. "Just when you touched me. That's why you were sucked into the void as well." They thought everyone knew not to touch demons for this very reason. But here was Percival, surprising them once again. The furious fire in his eyes, too, was quite a surprising sight in a merperson.

"Well, send me back. I'm too old to be in a cold spot like this."

Larimar glanced at Anemone, who had knelt on the floor to secure a camera inside a backpack. "Can you exorcise him?"

"Larry, dear, you know the rules. You can't go home before the job is done, and the pentagram needs to charge. My boat is leaving in an hour. I don't have time to wait here with you."

"But... Percival isn't supposed to be here."

She shrugged. "You'll have to make the best of it. It's been months since my last expedition and I've been looking forward to this a lot."

"Expedition?" Percival sputtered. "How long will you be gone?"

"Just three days," Anemone replied. "It's kind of funny. I'll be observing maritime wildlife and here I have a real merman in my very own house!"

"Anemone is a documentary filmmaker," Larimar grumbled. "She always needs someone to watch over her plants while she's gone. And for some reason, that someone is me."

"Well, I tried working with earth demons but they make such a mess. And the boy next door forgets to water my flowers half the time!"

"You can't go!" Percival bristled. "I demand to be sent home immediately."

"Sorry," Anemone said. "I do have a luxurious bathtub, if it's any help. Gotta dash now!" She picked up her backpack and the other two bags that had been lying around, gave Larimar and Percival a little wave, and rushed out the front door into the fog.

For an awkwardly long moment, Percival and Larimar just stared at each other.

"I can carry you up to the bathroom," Larimar offered finally, awkwardly braiding and unbraiding three of their tentacles.

"And what would I do there? Where will *you* go?" Percival

9

asked suspiciously.

"I'll be at work in the greenhouse." Larimar hesitated. "I suppose it's a little warmer in there..."

"Then take me there," Percival ordered. "There's a reason why I live in a heated part of the ocean, you know."

"I know. You're old and you can afford it."

Larimar cringed as Percival's glare intensified.

"I mean, that's why *I* live there. I was joking..."

"You wouldn't be joking if you had a rheumatic tail yourself! Do you have any idea how much worse it feels outside of the water? What's the air thinking, being so ridiculously cold? It'll be bad enough not having any painkrillers here!"

Before guilt could creep up on Larimar, a solution popped into their mind. "Wait here."

"What did you think I was going to do? Crawl around like a sea cucumber?"

But Larimar had already hurried to Anemone's laundry room. A minute later, they returned with a white laundry basket on wheels. They lifted Percival and had to support themselves with two of their hind tentacles in order not to keel over. It was easy to forget how much heavier things were on land, and Percival wasn't exactly as slender as the merpeople usually depicted in human art. But Larimar managed to put him down relatively gently, and then held their flippers over the basket to flood it with warm water.

Percival didn't look impressed. "This thing has holes. Large ones. It's not going to contain the water!"

Larimar rolled their eyes. "I'm a water demon. I *control* water. And its temperature, so if you're complaining too much..."

"Fine," Percival growled. "But if you're so good at keeping water in place, why are you dripping on the carpet?"

Larimar ignored the question, pretending they needed all

10

their focus to fill the merman's makeshift mobile bath.

Once the water came higher than his teal tail, Percival closed his eyes for a moment, relief clear on his face.

"You're welcome," Larimar said triumphantly, hooking a tentacle over the edge of the basket and pulling it behind themselves, down the corridor and out the back door.

How had Percival ever thought that being on land was pleasant? He had such fond memories of long days on the beach, basking in the sun or enjoying the tickle of cool rain on his skin. Surely he was remembering it wrong. Probably because he'd been in such good company at the time.

Not that Larimar was so awful, and being here was a lot more acceptable now that Percival's bones were warmed and his muscles relaxed. But still. Being on land had been better with Gim. So had being in the water, and even, on one silly afternoon when they'd been imitating flying whales, being in the air.

He huffed. This was why he never came out anymore. It was always a disappointment.

Except, he had to admit, Anemone's greenhouse was quite impressive. It was a sea of green reaching as far as Percival could see, lush and fresh, touching his farmer's heart. Before he'd retired, he'd been very successful at growing his favorite seaweed: *Pyropia tenera*, or as most merpeople knew it, gim. Customers from all over the ocean had shown up, noticing with how much passion and love Percival cultivated the weed. After all, it shared its name with his husband.

Gim, on the other hand, had always felt more connected to animals than to plants. He'd been a trainer of pets like Rhumba, as well as working fish like the ones who pulled the public chariots. Sadly, Gim's ichness had progressed too quickly to finish Rhumba's training, but Percival had kept the catfish anyway. Taking it to another trainer would have felt like giving away the last piece of Gim's legacy. He couldn't have borne the thought.

Percival was jerked back to the present as Larimar took a sharp turn into the next row of vegetables. They were still dragging him along, slither-walking on their tentacles, and holding out their flippers to send a soft but steady rain over the greens.

Percival wished he could comment on how the plants were treated or give some kind of advice based on his own experiences, just to have something to say. But as the plants were all thriving, the silence stretched on.

In the end, he settled on a question.

"So this is what you do every time you're away, huh? Water plants?"

Larimar tilted their head. "It's not exactly my most impressive task. My duties vary a lot. There's the obvious ones, like extinguishing fires, building and taking down dams, stopping monsoons, you know. Facing down the occasional rogue fire demon. But sometimes people have silly requests, like Anemone. Or like that one person who invited me to their kid's birthday party in order to provide them with a water slide."

"Can they really think of no other way to solve those things than summoning a demon?" Percival asked incredulously.

Larimar shrugged.

"And you can never refuse?"

"I can, if I can convince them I have a really good reason. Like, I don't want to destroy things just to bring destruction, and I don't want to endanger anyone. That kindness, as humans call it, makes me a pretty popular demon."

"So that's why you're away so often," Percival muttered, trying to hide his pout when Larimar looked back at him.

"It's not really often, compared to how it used to be," they

12

said. "We used to be summoned all the time, but these days most land people don't believe in demons anymore. And since you waterfolk see us around all the time, you're not that impressed with demon magic. Now and then I'm called in to clean a lagoon, but other than that I don't get much local work."

"If the humans *are* impressed with your magic, why do they pay you in spinach? I mean, you don't even like spinach. You're always offering it to me. For which I'm grateful, because it's delicious, but..."

Larimar stopped next to a pepper plant, tangling and untangling their tentacles rapidly.

"I may have lied about hating it. And getting too much of it." They avoided Percival's gaze. "Anemone gave it to me once because she'd just invested in another documentary and didn't really have anything else to settle the bill with. I accepted, because she'd paid well in the past, and for all I complain, this is an easy job. And... I'd only just moved to my new house. I was looking for a way to start talking to the good-looking merman next door." They glanced up, smiling a little, and Percival huffed out a laugh.

"Right. Good-looking. If you're into wrinkles and flabs..."

"I may not show it, but compared to me, you're still young," Larimar said. "You were growing all that seaweed in your backyard so I thought you might want to try some other green leaf. And then it turned out you loved it, so I acted like summoners were always giving it to me because of some silly demon myth."

Percival frowned. "So you *asked* for it instead of actual payment? For *me*?"

Larimar started walking and watering again, entering a row that housed flowers more colorful than anything Percival had ever seen on land. "I'm living in my dream house these days. I couldn't think of much else I needed pearls for, and as for other treasures, I'm happy with my sea glass. At least the spinach was

13

an excuse to talk to you."

"I thought you were always too busy to talk."

"I thought you were feeling obligated to make small talk with your needy new neighbor, and indulged me only because you were being polite."

"I was going to ask you in for tea," Percival blurted out, surprised to hear the words come out of his own mouth. "But then we ended up here."

Larimar stopped again and turned to stare at him, water still pouring out over a yellow-flowered plant with little purplish hairs on its vesicles. "I was trying to get inside before I could invite you to come look at my glass collection. You probably didn't want me to bore you with that."

"Bore me? It sounds fascinating!"

Larimar's gills colored a little mauve. "You may regret saying that when we get home."

"I doubt I will."

"Well... That's a date." Larimar's color grew even more intense and Percival couldn't help grinning.

And then he gasped as a sharp, awful pain spread in his left shoulder.

"Percival!"

Larimar stared at him in shock. On the spot where, a moment ago, they'd been watering a perfectly harmless plant, a monster had risen. And one of its enlarged vesicles had clamped around Percival's shoulder like an enormous maw.

This was why demons usually worked alone: distractions could have horrible consequences. Talking about an actual date with Percival had made Larimar so delightedly nervous that they must have accidentally fertilized the plant, making it grow impossibly fast. And now it could cost them all the beautiful opportunities that had opened up just moments ago.

"Do something!" Percival gritted out, his face scrunched up in pain.

Larimar tried with both flippers and tentacles, but couldn't pull the plant off Percival's shoulder. Its sharp hairs, now as long as tentacles, had pierced Percival's flesh, holding on fast. Then Larimar felt something against their right flipper.

They barely pulled away in time to avoid getting stuck themselves.

"Distract it!" Percival cried. "It's an *Utricularia*. Bladderwort. Find something small. Something it can try to eat instead of *me*!"

Larimar looked around frantically. "Like a flower?"

"No! It's carnivorous!"

"Wait. A bug!" Larimar clapped their flippers together and between them, a beetle-shaped piece of ice appeared, wriggling its little legs. "Go on," they said as they offered it to the bladder around Percival's shoulder. "Ice bugs are *much* tastier than merman!"

It worked. The plant retracted its tentacles and snapped shut around the ice. Larimar ran, pushing the laundry basket and trying not to trip over their own tentacles.

They didn't stop until they reached the glass wall farthest from the *Utricularia*, leaning a flipper against it as they tried to catch their breath.

"Good thinking."

"Thank you." Percival studied his right shoulder, which bore purple marks. "Why does that Anemone even own those monster plants?"

"She doesn't..." Larimar didn't meet his eyes. "I've gone a little overboard with my magic. And the plant's hunger grew as much as its size. I'm sorry."

15

"Well, I'm still alive," Percival said. "She should take it to a fair. That sure is the largest *Utricularia longeciliata* anyone has ever seen, if I'm to believe my books on human floriculture. In fact, they did warn about aquatic *Utricularia* species eating small fish. No wonder it went wild when it saw me."

Larimar smiled. "I can't blame it, either," they said, making Percival snort. "It'll go back to normal. Hopefully before I need to tend to it again."

The plant seemed to have shrunk a little already. At this rate, the ice bug might fall out of its bladder before it was digested – it would soon be too large for the *Utricularia* to hold onto.

"I don't know about you, but I could really use a cup of tea after all that." Percival shifted in the laundry basket. "It's not my house, but since we'll be stuck here for days, we might as well have that date? If you like?"

"You'll still call it a date?" Larimar seldom showed all their pointy teeth because it tended to unsettle people, but now they couldn't help grinning. "Even after I set a murderous plant on you?"

"You're a demon. For all I know, that might be a declaration of love," Percival deadpanned, and Larimar chuckled.

"Yes. Let's go with that."

They pulled the basket back into the house, where they opened several cupboards at once with their tentacles. "I always forget where she keeps the tea. Have you ever had *Camellia sinensis*? Land-tea?"

"Only read about it," Percival replied as Larimar filled two cups with a swish of their flippers and then fumbled to fill some infusers with dry leaves.

"Three days..." Percival mused as he took his cup and a cookie from Larimar. "It's a good thing Rhumba knows how to look after itself. Though I'm afraid it will have made a mess of your roses by the time we'll get back."

"That's okay. My neighbor's good with plants, so I'll make him restore them," Larimar teased. In truth, the roses barely survived underwater even with their magic's help, but it was worth it. And perhaps Percival *did* have some good tips.

Percival hummed. "As long as you provide that handsome neighbor of yours with an extra warm bath afterwards."

"Nice change, having someone carry out tasks for *me* in exchange for rewards," Larimar mused. "I might summon you more often."

"Deal."

Larimar laughed. Talking to Percival was so much easier now that they weren't fretting about how to ask him out. Perhaps this really *could* work.

"We should have done this much earlier," they said, sipping the tea. It was the perfect temperature, of course, and would stay that way even if they forgot about it.

"We should have. But at least we summoned our courage in the end." Percival raised his cup to them and smiled.

The house was very quiet when Anemone returned. Perhaps too quiet. She wondered if the demon had found a way to get home before finishing the job. Surely not. If they had, they wouldn't have been able to return, and that might be disastrous for her plants. Besides, it might be for the best if Larry had been stuck with the old merman all this time. Obviously, wooing him with spinach hadn't gotten the message across yet. And sure, she'd been glad that Larry had become more motivated to work for her than they'd ever been when she paid them in pearls, but seeing them with Percival, she'd realized it was starting to get ridiculous.

However, if they *were* still here, forced to talk to each other at last, why couldn't she hear them?

She went to check in the greenhouse, but they weren't there. Everything seemed to have been watered recently, though, and the tomatoes looked particularly tasty. The bladderwort somehow even seemed to have grown twice as large as it had been. Only her spinach was in a pitiable state. She shouldn't have been surprised. After all, the merman had to eat and *he* wasn't bound to any demonic contracts.

The merman... Of course. There really was only one place where they could be.

She opened the bathroom door very slowly, trying not to make a sound, but Larimar immediately lifted their head from where it had been resting on Percival's chest in the long whirlpool tub.

"Huh?" Percival said, blinking awake and making the water splash as he scrambled to sit upright.

"Oh, you two are adorable!" Anemone squeed. "I'm not interrupting anything, am I?"

"We were just taking a nap." Larimar leaned back and stretched their flippers, spraying more water over the side of the bath. "We've earned it. Percival made sure your plants are doing better than ever."

"So I saw. Does this mean that I'm getting both of you next time as well?"

Percival was blushing violet, but he smiled, and that was quite a change from the scowl she'd gotten from him when he arrived in the pentagram. He looked at least ten years younger. "You might," he said. "After all, we do make a good team."

Anemone giggled. Her next expedition was already being

arranged, but she'd leave the plants to the boy next door for once. There was no way she'd call Larimar away from home anytime soon.

MINERVA CERRIDWEN is a Belgian writer and pharmacist. Her first published work was the short story "Match Sticks" in queer fairy tale anthology *Unburied Fables*. Her novella *The Dragon of Ynys* came out in 2018. For updates on her newest projects, check out her website minervacerridwen.wordpress. com or follow her on Twitter @minerva_cerr.

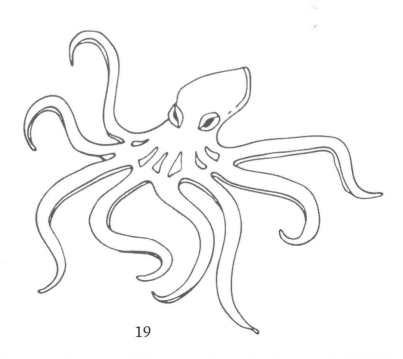

WORLDS BETWEEN US

by Riley Sidell

Courtship across planets was difficult. Inu had lived apart from girlfriends in the past, but not half a year at a time. Every summer, the pod migrated north and she was alone with her whales for the season. In their two years together – on this world anyway – she and Anika had only been apart for a few weeks, when they were testing the time difference between the fairy homeworld and her own.

Six months apart sounded like forever.

Anika's sunset-yellow wings took on a poisonous hue in the violent green light of the portal to her home world. She didn't seem worried by the prospect of hopping around the stars this way. Nothing seemed to worry her. Inu had fallen between worlds twice, and both times were accidental.

"The months will fly by," Anika said. "Might be seven if we don't have the time difference right. Three weeks for me is going to feel like an eternity."

Anika shuffled along the cave floor, inching closer to where Inu lounged at the water's edge. She offered a small, soft hand. Instinct jerked Inu's own hands to her chest. Her dislike of touch was different than the natural wariness of most mer. Some thought touch between lovers should lead to sex, at least at some point. Though Inu was a sex-averse asexual, Anika was indifferent to it. Both had broken up with girlfriends over it. What a match they were. It was comforting to have someone who understood her sexuality, almost like fate.

And yet Inu's hands still trembled. Fingers interlaced with Anika's, Inu pulled her close. Would Anika come back? Was it worth it to play with time like this? *Could* she come back, or did this magic have an expiration date?

Too long out of the water made Inu's skin tight and dry. She wasn't comfortable using her lungs this much. When they usually spent time together, Anika would conjure great bubbles, sink to the lower levels of Inu's underwater home of Insipan, and race her through the bright avenues among schools of brilliant fish the size of Inu's eyeteeth.

In her mind, Inu could feel Anika's nose wrinkle with a smile. She made certain she wasn't sharing her thoughts with the fairy curled up in her lap. And also melted, just a little.

"Can I show you something before you go?" Inu said.

"Only if you want to."

Calling the memory was faster than blinking. Comforting heat grew behind Inu's eyes, radiating down each of her four arms to her fingertips and into the side of Anika's face, her hand, the soft folds of her stomach.

Anika leaned against the doorway of her glittering home, wings lit up like fire against the setting sun. She shouted back indoors – perhaps to her fathers or apprentice. By the time Inu surfaced to listen, Anika's attention had turned to her: the nervous girl lurking in a magical glass bowl in her garden. The nervous girl whose skin went hot when Anika's eyes met hers. That smile could have stopped Inu's heart.

Anika pulled away, breaking from the memory and returning them to the grotto.

"I wish I could show you my memories too. Dad might know of a spell, but knowing him it's been tucked under a floorboard for a decade." Her gaze drifted to the craggy ceiling as she muttered, "Hiding a portal spell on the back of a pie recipe. That man."

The translation spell Anika had cast, good as it was, did not tell Inu what 'floorboard' meant. Probably some kind of fairy secret.

For the millionth time she considered asking Anika to stay and plan the festival here. If Anika stayed, Inu could put this off a week, a month. Shelve this worry for later.

"I love you," Inu said, voice soft and a little raspy.

"I love you too."

Anika's tone was earnest, though tension crept in the edges of her voice, sharpening it. Inu couldn't imagine planning a solstice festival for an entire city.

While Inu worried, Anika busied herself with checking the portal, disappearing behind it a few times. Inu fought against the quiver in her stomach, made her best attempt at a flippant tone as she said, "We should be back near Insipan before you, though Medyuu would have us stay in the tropics forever. The squid there are lazier than he is." She tried to fake a casual smile.

Anika's soft wings drew closer to her body. She wasn't buying it. Inu had never been this person, this *nervous*. All four of her hands quivered, the upper two gesticulating more than usual while the lower pair rummaged in her bag. Would Anika remember the significance of the pendants? One way to find out.

"Look, I, ah, nicked this for you – I didn't steal it, alright, I can hear your wings being all angry over there. Belu made it. It's not that big of a deal," Inu said, voice trailing to a whisper.

Thrusting her open palm before her, the pendant flew from Inu's unsteady hand and hit the portal behind Anika. The symbol of her eternal love for her girlfriend disappeared from the world to a pair of gasps, presumably landing safely in Anika's garden in Nasa'im.

Anika met Inu's horrified gaze with a soft touch on the forearm. "Whatever it was, thank you. I didn't think to get you anything. That's awful of me."

Oh.

She didn't know what it was. Hadn't seen it.

A kiss to Inu's cheek only buried the worry for later. Anika lingered inches from Inu's face, lips parted to reveal a hint of razor-sharp teeth, as if there were words caught between them.

As much as they tried, kisses could not stop time, and had to end when Inu scratched at her dry skin. The portal was an unbearably hot reminder that this moment could not last forever.

"I should go," Anika whispered. "Take care."

"Say hello to your dads for me," Inu said.

"Pay Belu back for me."

With a mock scowl, Inu slipped back into the water, scrubbing her scalp with the pads of her fingers, desperate to stop the tingly tight feeling at the roots of her hair.

Within reach of the portal, Anika stood on tiptoe to begin the dance of her magic, her fingers carving bright symbols into the air around her, each one fading just as it flashed to life. Magic like that didn't exist in the sea, though if it ever had, it would have rotted away centuries ago like the land, passing out of the memories of even the oldest creatures.

It seemed too unpredictable, too wild. What if it went wrong? If she drew the wrong rune? As much as it frightened her, Inu loved to watch Anika's magic. Just that morning she had turned a gray stone brilliant pink with a few flicks of her wrist.

24

The last rune was split in twain, brought to either side of the portal. In a single movement, Anika drew her hands together, twisted around, and stepped backward into her home. The round portal became a thin oval, a bright line, then vanished.

The grotto went dark as the deepest trenches. Inu stayed until the stone walls turned cold.

Inu went to see Belu one last time before the pod began its migration to the tropics. Preferring the quiet of the open sea, he lived in the shallow waters above the wide deep-sea trenches that laced the world. With the aid of a dozen tools and the pinching strength of his claws, his calloused hands worked glowing molten glass into beautiful, twisting swirls.

While her friend worked, Inu hunted the seabed nearby for sparkling treasures, keeping clear of the toxic clouds spewed forth by the hydrothermal vents. Her arms were overladen with gems and ore and a miscellany of glittering things while she told Belu what had happened with the pendant. Belu's lobster charges scuttled around, hiding in the chill of Inu's shadow when she paused.

"What if Anika doesn't know what it was? What if she forgot—"

"If you told her, she remembers," Belu said.

"She might not. She might not even find it. What if it got lost in space or, I don't know, *whatever*."

"Doubt it. You showed me the memory of when you told her mer give pendants to their partners. I think she knew what it was, and I think even if she didn't recognize it before you nearly took her eye out, she will know as soon as she finds it."

Inu fiddled with a stone. "So why not say something? She didn't say anything."

"Did you ever consider that she might be as nervous as you are?"

She grumbled.

Belu was quiet a moment, focused on reheating the glass to a more malleable state. How he managed the tongs at such a distance, Inu had no idea. She stopped picking through the sand to watch him work. One of Belu's lobsters zoomed past her tail, brushing against her flukes. It purred, zoomed past again. Inu scratched it behind the eye stalks, eliciting a purr so vigorous her fingers vibrated. Finally, she was too uncomfortable in the silence to keep quiet.

"Do you have anything blue?" he asked.

Glad to be rid of that conversation, Inu sighed, dumped her armfuls of trinkets onto the stone opposite Belu's workbench. The pile of castoffs rustled in the gentle current, twinkling like so many stars. Belu stopped working on the glass, instead leaning over his workbench to scrutinize her choices. Inu picked through her findings and held them up in turn while he directed them into separate piles.

"No. No. That's part of a lobster claw, Inu, that's disgusting. Throw that out. Wait, what was that last one?"

Inu scrabbled for the gem she had already tossed into the 'no' pile. "This? It looks like it was an eyeball once."

Inu tossed the claw over her shoulder, relinquished the eye. It leered at her from the workbench as she rummaged through the castoffs, a reminder that she hadn't hunted in months. Everything that crossed her lips since had been purchased from a market already dead, occasionally prepared by Inu's sister. Anika couldn't stand the wriggling, could hardly stomach the chill of the things she could bear to swallow.

Fairies ate everything hot and charred, all of it long dead before it passed their lips. None of it tasted nice. Inu's stomach

26

lurched in protest at the thought of more bread.

She had been a great hunter once. Could she lose that too?

Both moons had grown full and waned to slivers before Inu and her pod were in the heart of the tropics. It was the last year before the pod's only calf would migrate south to live with the other males in colder waters. Liroosa, his mother, was distressed. Nose pointed to the sky, the great whale had been trying to sleep for an hour but would jolt awake with stress just as she began to relax.

"Medyuu is too small to be without a pod." Liroosa's distressed chirps drew a deep, warbling note of complaint from the depths. The podmother's worry was distracting the pod from the hunt.

Inu's response took longer to formulate, as whales had no words for time. Dancing around that came naturally, at least when she spent every moment with them. Speaking to Anika more than her whales meant she had fallen out of practice of thinking timelessly.

A fat bubble of air burbled from Inu's lips as she sighed, tickling her nose. Another habit picked up from fairies. "He may find kinship in the icy waters. He may be the sort that swims between pods. There's no way to know."

"But he is so small."

"Medyuu is grown, and a good hunter. I am smaller than he is, and I survive just fine."

"It's not the same. Inu has a pod."

Inu grumbled in her native mer language. Not wanting to do another circuit in this conversation today, Inu clicked, using echolocation to look for the pod below. Nothing in her range, though a pair of hunters answered on their way up with the prey they were herding toward her.

Liroosa joined in, as her range of echolocation was greater. Thrummed a laugh so deep, the bass made Inu's own lungs shake. "Good luck."

Inu arced backward and dove for the darkness and her dinner, relying on the bursts of echolocation rather than her eyes, which were no help in low light. If Inu chose, she could survive on fish and octopus – creatures that lived at a pressure she could handle. But squid made her feel close to the pod, and hunting kept her mind from things that made her hands shake.

It was a matter of pride to take a squid down unaided. Inu hadn't needed a blade in years. Her teeth and mind were sharp enough. She was a match for squid.

Most squid.

Inu tore after the creature with a vengeance. It was young, no larger than her. She creaked at it as she followed it down into the dark where it may have felt at home, had the darkness not been alive with the bright clicks of a dozen hungry whales.

Before she could lay tooth on it, the squid escaped into the absolute dark. It was too quick, and Inu could go no deeper without harm. She was neither sturdy nor whale enough for a miles-deep dive.

She ascended to a comfortable depth and paused to call to the pod. A groan sounded from the deep. Close enough for Inu to be tugged by their turbulence, two whales rocketed past from the depths, headed for fresh breaths at the surface. They should've been able to hold their breath longer than that.

A massive, writhing silhouette rose from the darkness. Fear sent Inu rushing for her whale; it was not uncommon for a squid to attach itself to the great, blocky heads of her charges in desperate attempts to drown them. The whale clicked low – a reassuring sound meant for a worried Inu. The silhouette solidified. She was chasing a horde of squid, all of them small.

Black tendrils bloomed from the heart of the swarm as they inked and scattered. One made the mistake of brushing past Inu in its panic. She creaked to locate the squid in the cloud, teeth bared, eyes closed. With hungry fingers, she grasped the end of its tentacle. The squid squirmed in pain, spewed a jet of water in Inu's face as it emptied its siphon to rocket away. It shot off, tearing its own tentacle to escape her. Seawater laced with ink and blood slipped between her snarling teeth, filled her to the tip of her flukes with a viciousness she hadn't felt in months.

Oh, that *blood*.

Not until the tips of her fingers brushed the fleeing squid's tentacle a second time did Inu realize how much she'd missed this. Needed it. Nervous trembling became strength and speed, fueling the hunger, the need.

A high, rapid burst of clicks startled the panicked squid toward the light, Inu in ravenous pursuit, blood upon her tongue, nerves alight with adrenaline. The squid rounded on her. Foolish.

All teeth and claws and hot instinct, Inu reached for the squid as its monstrous arms snatched at her. Like a good whale, she flipped, her tail toward its head, her own head toward its tentacles. She stared into its great, wide eye as its suckers snatched her hair, tentacles wound around her armpit.

It screeched, its beak clicking rage and pain at this girl, this upset to the cycle of life. The mer girl was silent. Words were useless. It was startled enough, thrashing in her grasp. She had already won.

One of Inu's lower hands grasped the underside of its mantle as another grasped its body just above its eyes. Her upper pair of hands clawed the tentacles that came for her eyes and those her claws missed met her sharp and angry teeth. The squid's flesh pulsed a mottled white with stress, the patches dancing as she

29

slapped its head with the flat of her tail.

No matter her hunger, she pitied it. She would give it the peace it was owed. Inu was a hunter, not a monster. Familiar warmth flowed down her throat and through her fingertips as she passed her memory to the squid.

Nothing could harm her here. There was nothing here to worry her. Belly full, pod cared for and dozing just beneath her, it was safe. Not a cloud in the sky.

Inu bobbed atop the gentle waves, flat on her back, the summer sun warming her stomach. She yawned.

Lazy fingers traced the pale circular scars marking her a hunter, a good Guardian.

Peace. Calm. This is where she belonged.

She breathed in, held it in her lungs. Slow breath out and she thought of nothing at all. Instead, she drifted in and out of dreamless sleep, lulled by the distant crash of whitecaps.

Nothing could harm her.

She tore the brain free, swallowing it whole. The texture was gritty and made her skin crawl. Inu allowed the memory to drain away, leaving her alone with the squid's corpse. Only then did she disentangle the tentacle from her hair. It danced beneath her hands even in death.

Disassembling the rest of the squid was simple. A pair of hands split the mantle along its length, exposing the massive creature's innards. Inu savored her favorite bits first: eyes, heart, radula, gills. The eyes were best when she could fit one in her mouth whole and intact. It popped, flooding her tongue with the taste of victory.

A careful swipe of her claws along the inside of the mantle separated the unsavory remainders from the squid's delectable flesh. Most mer might not hunt their own dinners, at least not anymore, but Inu was neither whale nor mer but something else entirely. She was Inu.

Cautious and skilled as she was with the disembowelment, a hasty slice punctured the ink sac in the squid's head and spoiled the rest of its innards with its stain. Inu swore. She could've sold that ink in Insipan for enough clams to keep her sister up to her eyes in jewels and her tutting to a minimum. Inu hissed, found her lungs less full than she would like, and sang into the depths for help. Her gills would suffice, but she was tired. She missed the sun, the wind on her skin. "Air. Please" Rising to the surface too quickly would make her sick. Though she held the contaminated innards away from her body she could still taste the bitter twang of ink on her tongue.

Medyuu came to her rescue. Sweet little Medyuu, last calf born to the pod and now a grown whale. He said nothing, only hovered in space, waiting for her to drift closer to him and slip the leaking entrails into his mouth. Not too close. She didn't touch his wrinkled back, not even when he blew a great stream of bubbles for her to breathe. The fetid, stale air made her retch, though not even the taste of vomit at the back of her throat could sour this day.

"Are you okay, little mer?" he said.

"Yeah. Thank you."

She had tasted worse. Breathed worse. He trailed her to the surface, keeping a respectful distance. Inu had shown him memories when he was a calf. It wasn't strange with children. Now he was grown, due to leave, and she preferred to keep her self to herself.

At night the sky was never truly dark. The moons loomed above like watchful eyes in a face freckled with stars. Dancing around in the light of one of those stars was Anika, though Inu was not sure which star it was. Inu hadn't thought of her all day. Guilt gnawed at her gut. Beneath her, half the pod slept like massive weeds, noses pointed toward the skies in a manner that would be eerie were it not familiar. She was glad to not be prey.

The whales who'd woken earlier breached against waves twice their height, filling the air with glimmering spray. Exhausted, Inu floated on her side. One eye watched the whales soar above the surface and the other caught their bubble trails as they curved back into the deep.

A light flared to life on the edge of her vision. It was brilliant yellow, unnatural in the way it lingered, static against the waves, disappearing only when the troughs fell below its light. She couldn't think of a creature in the sea that glowed so bright in the darkness, had never heard any podmates mention such a monster.

It was dangerously near the edge of the trench; more than once she was dragged near the cliffs that bordered the deep ocean, threatening to carve fresh scars.

Medyuu sang her name.

"I'm fine," she said. "I couldn't sleep."

He fell quiet. He was up to something, but he was grown now. She was no longer in charge of his well-being. Knowledge didn't silence the worry. Medyuu's disappearance eastward did not silence the worry.

The light lengthened to a line that grew larger the nearer she swam. Curious. Slowing to a hard-won standstill against the pull of the high tide waves, she clicked at the light and saw nothing. Somehow it was immune to echolocation. It did not exist.

She was glad to be alone once she realized once what it was. Inu circled it to be sure, keeping clear of the cliffs. The line of light grew broad and split, becoming oblong as she faced the portal head-on.

A distinctly frazzled Anika looked out of the portal's field of view, distracted by something else. Just there, now, months ahead of schedule. Inu counted backward on her fingers. The days had blurred together; she had been keeping track of time only in relation to Medyuu's departure, not Anika's return.

Inu set off a flurry of clicks, tugged her hair to be sure this was no dream. The abnormal, round void in the vision verified yes, this was real. More than that, there was a familiar figure not far away.

"You should be asleep," she said to Medyuu. "Your mother worries."

It was difficult to convey annoyance to whales. Whales did not care. Having been found out, Medyuu clicked back at her, as though he could not see her in the half-dark, had not been following her. He was a terrible actor.

"I needed a breath," he said, and left her alone.

Engrossed in whoever she was speaking to across the stars in Nasa'im, Anika did not spot Inu, even when Inu was near enough to count every yellow feather of her wings. This wasn't how portals worked. They were opaque, not windows, and yet there was Anika. A wave drew Inu up, away from the portal. She fought it, dove, gripped the portal's strange edges and held tight. It was hot. Too hot, but Inu could not let go.

Inu tapped the portal's face with her thumbs. "Anika? Are you really there?"

Anika startled in slow motion. Wings flared, her face lit up. Her mouth moved and, though Inu could feel the vibrations of her voice in her fingertips, the sound meant nothing.

The translation spell they used had worn off. Of course it had. Anika had been gone for months. Inu's heart sank.

"Ani. Anika." No response. Inu tapped the hard surface of the portal again. "Anika!"

The fairy paused, mouth open, brows knit in confusion.

"I can't understand you. You probably can't understand me either. The spell doesn't work anymore."

Anika was already at work, hands trailing magic through the air. It was lengthy, and longer still at the pace she could move. At the spell's close, Anika's fingertips hit the surface of the portal where one of Inu's palms rested. She leaned in, tucked her short-cropped hair behind her ear.

"Did it work? I don't– I don't think it worked. Magic won't work if you can't touch something, right?" Inu waited for an answer. "Right. Guess not."

They frowned at each other. Inu cracked a smile before Anika caught up with her.

"What is that?" Medyuu's curious clicks startled her. Inu assumed he had gone back to the pod, but of course not. He was a few meters behind her, beady eye watching.

"Magic. Didn't you leave?"

"Making sure Inu is not swallowed by sharks while shouting at circles."

A tap on the window-portal drew Inu's attention before she could grumble at her whale. Anika brushed aside the collar of her shirt to reveal the pendant Inu had tried to give her all those months ago, the pendant that had haunted her ever since. It dangled from a fine chain, the stone glinting violet. Inu's heart leapt.

Anika's face softened as she said... something. A slow, earnest something.

It was hard to not let her frustration show. Inu growled low in her throat. She had grown too used to understanding, to certainties. Perhaps they had leaned too hard on magic to speak to each other.

Before she could respond, Anika was drawn away, perhaps

back to the festival. The portal disappeared, leaving Inu with bright spots behind her closed eyes, alone with Medyuu in the growing dawn.

"That is your mate," he said. Not a question.

"Partner, yeah. Not into the mate thing. I don't know if she remembers what pendants are for. I'm surprised you do. You don't listen to anything."

Medyuu was quiet for a moment. Then: "I know everything. She knows, too."

Inu sighed. Medyuu whale-laughed at her, trilling a low note that made her grin.

"I know," she said. "I shouldn't worry as much as I do."

"Are you worrying about worrying?"

"Not anymore," she said. Poked at a barnacle near Medyuu's mouth, which he dodged as expected. "Let's go hunt."

Half-asleep with only her eyes above the water's surface, Inu watched the portal blossom. For real this time, not a dream, not like the hundred times she'd checked the grotto after the pod returned to the seas near Insipan. Anika was back. She was here.

Inu surfaced while Anika drew a spell in the air, carried it down the stilted slope into the sea, and pressed it to her forehead.

"Your wings are getting wet. Should've made the bubble first."

Anika pulled a fist from her pocket, opened it slightly so the sparkling something within could dangle in the light, shivering in her trembling grasp. A pendant on a fine chain.

Inu began a hundred sentences and abandoned them all.

"It's not as good as the one Belu made, but I tried. It's purple. Hard to tell in this light, though. Uh. The chains are rust proof, but I'll have to refill the spell every few months. I hope you like it." Anika fiddled with the chain, eyes darting between Inu and the wall behind her. "Partners? I'm sorry, I don't know how—"

Inu's mouth crashed into Anika's like a wave meeting the sea. This was home. This was real. Shaking fingers fumbled to clasp the pendant round her neck. Forehead to forehead, breaking to breathe: "I love it."

RILEY SIDELL is a queer writer of fantasy stories, an average knitter, and the human of one cat. Riley tweets @RileySidell and blogs at rileysidell.wordpress.com.

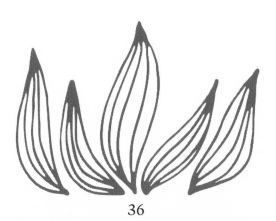

COLOR AND PRESSURE

by Evvan Burke

Colored lights flashed and danced across Liam Hardy's face as he sat on the hard bench, staring out the twenty-five-foot-wide, curved window of the submarine.

"Hardy," someone called. Liam turned around to see Naida, one of his co-workers and fellow deep-sea diver, waving from the upper deck with a faint purple glow striking her face. She glanced over both her shoulders and slid under the guard rail to his level.

"Did you forget the dive program is suspended until these things leave? Or were you just enjoying the show?" she asked, sitting down next to him.

Liam chuckled dryly, something closer to a cough than a real laugh. She was right to rib him. The dive deck was usually full of technicians and divers like themselves, preparing to venture outside the submarine to collect samples of aquatic life at the depths of the ocean. For the last few days, however, the dive program had been suspended as a safety precaution. He had been alone for the last two hours.

The creatures swimming outside were pale white blobs with wing-like fins spread about their bodies, like the petals of two roses facing away from one another. More striking, however, was the bioluminescence they produced, which Virgil Hooke – the reclusive deep-sea biologist in residence – theorized was a form of communication. Each creature emitted a powerful glow from the tips of their fins in constantly changing colors.

The creatures ranged in size from one to five feet, with the exception of one slightly further off that would have dwarfed the window if it were any closer. At least twenty feet long and emanating a soft, white light, it twirled forward as its fins swayed lazily like silk in the water, while the others bounced and swam energetically.

"It's amazing," Naida said, watching the creatures. "Ninety-five percent of the ocean had been unexplored before we came down here, and yet... I'm still surprised we could discover something like this."

"You didn't have faith in us?" Liam asked.

"Or the ocean. One or the other," she said, and then paused. "I noticed you and Dr. Hooke have been hanging out more. Good news?"

Liam hoped the colored lights would hide his blush. "It's not like that."

Naida rolled her eyes. "I don't know what else it could be. The man doesn't talk to anything without gills."

Liam turned away slightly, hiding the smile tickling his cheek. Naida often teased him about his relationship – or, so far, lack thereof – with Virgil, and he didn't need to give her any more reason to. Besides, he knew Virgil was perfectly happy talking to anyone, so long as they were willing to listen to him talk about his research.

"You know," she said, "he hasn't had lunch yet."

"How do you know?"

"He asked Dr. Kepper to bring it to him, but we agreed it

was better if you did. So I'd hop to it, if I were you. We both know he'd starve before leaving his lab. Or learn to filter feed, and then you'd never get him to move."

She stood up, her hand on his back gripping just enough shirt to pull him up with her.

"Alright, alright," he said, raising his hands in surrender. "I'll be Dr. Hooke's errand boy."

"Uh huh," Naida said dryly. She turned away, this time taking the stairs.

Liam followed, just slowly enough to let her get ahead of him. His hands were shaking, as they tended to do when the subject of Virgil came up. His therapist said it was a symptom of his general anxiety disorder, which was oddly disappointing.

General anxiety disorder. Nothing special. Just the sad, generic brand. Not worth the trouble it gave him.

But for the last few days, he had a good reason to be nervous. Ever since they'd closed the Dive Bay, he had been staking it out to find when it would be empty. And now, it was time to put Virgil's plan into action.

Dr. Virgil Hooke's laboratory was unlike the other labs on the *DSS Amphitrite* for two reasons. First and foremost, it held a large, cylindrical tank about three feet wide, rising from a metal base that kept it pressurized. Theo, a foot-long member of the same species that was currently surrounding their submarine, swam around inside the tank, shifting between content shades of blue-green.

Liam had found Theo a month or two after their undersea voyage began. They were a speck of color in the darkness Liam had scooped up to be identified by the scientists onboard, which soon became Virgil's pet project.

Originally, Virgil had named them Spec, short for Specimen, but Liam had objected. Spec was an abbreviation, not a name. Instead, Liam had suggested Theo, short for Theory, which had caught on despite its lack of technical accuracy.

The second strange thing was the bed pushed into a corner, which Virgil had moved out of his personal quarters their first week underwater. It also functioned as a makeshift desk, on which he currently sat cross-legged, staring at papers and making notes in a composition journal.

Like every room in the submarine, there were sunlamps attached to the walls, but the brightness bothered Theo, so Virgil preferred to keep them turned off. Instead, he worked using a reading light attached to the bedpost.

Liam set a plate of potatoes and meat substitute on the end of the bed, and glanced at one of the notebooks the scientist was working on. It was filled with drawings of the creatures that were outside, with various notations he couldn't understand scribbled in the margins.

"Still redacting?" he asked.

"Afraid so," Virgil said. He made one final note in his journal and then stood up. He walked to his actual desk, leaning close and squinting to read the spines of the books piled there. "Unfortunately, I was wrong on numerous aspects – nothing physiological, but it's clear we underestimated the social aspect."

With a sigh, Liam picked up the plate he had set on the bed and placed it on the desk, with a more audible clank.

"I thought Dr. Kepper was bringing me my lunch," Virgil said.

"I was voluntold," Liam said.

Virgil inspected his food with a scowl. "Do you think those potatoes were meant to be mashed or was it just a happy coincidence that they can be served that way?"

"I think it's what's for lunch," Liam said.

Virgil scoffed, but he grabbed the plate and took it back to his bed, poking at it with his fork. "Did your surveillance go as you'd hoped?"

Liam nodded. "It looks like tomorrow can go ahead as planned."

This reassured Virgil enough to take his first forkful as he descended into thought.

Liam sat on the other end of the bed, the papers an uncrossable moat between them. He watched Virgil eat, but quickly found himself distracted by Virgil's appearance. He had dark hair tied into a messy bun and copper skin that would have been a deeper, sunned brown if he hadn't sequestered himself away from the ship's sunlamps. He didn't have the wide shoulders or muscle Liam had, but his neatly tucked – if wrinkled – shirts and tapered pants fit attractively. He wore square wireframe glasses but still squinted from the lack of light, so the slight trace of crow's feet etched age into his otherwise youthful face.

"The pod may have some sort of hunting system which we're unaware of at the moment, but we won't have enough time to study it," Virgil said, snapping Liam back to attention.

"Don't they eat plankton or something?" Liam asked.

"Yes, they do."

"Not much hunting involved, is there?"

"There's a bit," Virgil said, putting down his fork. He preferred talking over eating anyways. "It's more like herding, to be fair. Using the currents to corral the plankton closer for a more efficient feeding."

"You'd think the plankton would learn," Liam said.

"Maybe," Virgil said. "With a few thousand years of evolution, perhaps."

Liam nodded, not quite understanding.

"We also dramatically underestimated their size," Virgil continued, absently taking another bite.

"You think they all grow to the size of a house?" Liam asked.

Virgil shrugged. "I don't see why not."

Liam glanced at the tank in the center of the room, and tried to imagine the behemoth outside swimming in it.

"So tomorrow," Virgil repeated, slowly.

"Yeah. The riskiest part will be sneaking the canister through," Liam said, referencing a two-foot glass cylinder that looked and functioned like a miniature model of the tank in the laboratory. The divers used them to take water samples, or carry deep-sea creatures onto the submarine.

"I'm more concerned with something else." Virgil turned to face Liam more completely, putting his plate on a chair. He swallowed a particularly difficult piece of potato before continuing. "It seems more logical that I be the one to do the dive."

The words went through Liam like a paper cut. "Absolutely not."

"Hear me out," Virgil said, making a pacifying gesture with his hands, but Liam powered through regardless.

"You've never dived before!"

Virgil scoffed. "I'm a marine biologist. I've been on a dive before."

"35,000 feet underwater?" Liam shouted. Virgil was momentarily silent.

"There will only be one of us there to operate the safety controls in case something goes wrong," Virgil said. "If anything happens, we won't have fifteen technicians on the deck to save us."

"Exactly," Liam said. "That's why I should be the one going out there."

"No, that's why I'm the one who should do it." His voice took on a hypnotic calmness, like white noise. "If something goes wrong, the odds of you saving my life are much higher than the other way around."

"I can teach you," Liam said. "You're brilliant. You'll pick it up."

"We have no time. And I'd freeze if it was a life or death situation."

Liam laughed humorlessly. "Do you think I'll be any better?"

"Now you're just being unfair to yourself."

But Liam could already feel his hands shaking against the bed. He had known he wasn't the right person to help Virgil from the beginning; too nervous, too cowardly. But he had wanted to be the right person because it was Virgil who was asking. Liam had enjoyed the idea of filling that role.

Now the thought made him pale. But Virgil was technically right. It was safer this way. Liam just didn't like who was taking on the extra risk.

"I'd understand," Virgil said, his words slow and forced but honest, "if you wanted to rescind your offer."

Guilt took a generous, acidic bite at Liam's heart.

"No," Liam said. "We do it tomorrow at 1400 hours, just as we planned."

Virgil exhaled, all at once letting go of stress that had been slowly gathering. Virgil crossed the divide and hugged him, his knees falling on some of his papers. He smelled like cinnamon body wash and eraser shavings.

"Thank you," Virgil said.

Liam moved his arms around Virgil self-consciously, then pulled him closer.

"Are you sure people won't see through this?" Virgil half-asked, half-predicted. Liam ignored him and continued walking. He'd borrowed a supply cart and hidden a canister under a tarp, surrounded by other tools. But he had to be careful. The pressure that made the container a viable environment for specimens also made it fragile. If anything struck it too hard, the entire thing would burst into too many wet shards of glass.

"No one should question anything if we act natural," Liam said. "Now lift with me."

Virgil sighed, but took his position opposite Liam. They lifted at a silent count of three and eased the cart over one of the submarine's many ledges, with only a slight rattle. Liam let out a breath, and realized his jaw had been tight up to the moment he had spoken. There was just one hallway and a corner before the Dive Bay now.

"Go on ahead and start up the machines. We should get you out as fast as possible," Liam said, slowly pushing the heavy cart to accelerate. Virgil nodded and jogged ahead. He was just about to turn the corner when he stopped, his poker face turning into Fifty-Two Pickup.

"Oh, hello Ms... Ms..." he stuttered.

Liam turned the corner and saw a person leap down from the ledge they had been perched on. "You can just call me Naida, Dr. Hooke. Everyone does. Now where would..." She looked around until she spotted Liam, who came to a halt with another worrying clank of glass.

"There you are," she said, smiling. "Got worried when you didn't show."

"Did we have plans?" Liam said, his voice steadier than his hands, but he gripped the cart tighter until his knuckles were bone.

"It's the last day they say we'll be with the pod. I assumed that meant you'd be here. But I suppose it also makes sense that you'd take the time to fetch Dr. Hooke," she said, gesturing to him. "This is his research, isn't it?"

Liam felt their lie reshaping itself in his mind like wet clay. "Yes, we're here to prepare for an experiment Dr. Hooke needs to perform. Timing being critical and all. While the research is still viable."

She nodded. "So this is more of a work thing than recreation?"

Liam nodded and glanced at Virgil, whose face was still a mess of half-expressed emotions. He tried to mentally will the man to join in, but Virgil just scurried ahead and disappeared into the room.

"You know," Naida said, "I'm free for the next few hours. If you'd like, I can help you and the good doctor run your tests. That way we can finish early and enjoy the last hours with the pod."

Liam's mind fumbled with their half-baked lie.

"Unless," she said, "this isn't about a test at all."

Liam glanced unconsciously toward where Virgil would be beyond the walls.

"Just be honest with me," Naida said. "There's a dive about to begin, isn't there?"

"What do you mean?" Liam said.

"Hey, it's a great idea," she said. "These creatures are the closest thing the good doctor has to an obsession. Brilliant. You offered him the chance to go out and see the pod up close and he jumped at the chance. Just promise me this: you're going to tell him, right?"

"Tell him what?" Liam asked.

"Tell him that you're interested," she said. "You've got a

perfect first date on your hands, but you have to tell him, or else it isn't a first date at all. It's just a nice thing. And nice things aren't worth a damn if they don't mean the same thing for everybody involved."

Liam breathed again. He tried to release his grip, only to find his hands were still shaking, and his mouth was dry. The hissing, creaking equipment of the submarine filled their silence.

"Tell me you're going to tell him," she said, "and I'll be out of your hair."

"Naida–," Liam said.

"I'm overstepping, I know," she said. "But you deserve this, Liam. You deserve to be happy. And maybe deserve a less-demanding friend."

Liam looked toward the wall again. The words froze in Liam's throat, like water down the wrong pipe, but he choked them out nonetheless. "Okay, I will."

She grabbed the cart, and Liam jumped, pulling it towards him reflexively.

"I saw nothing," she said, her serious tone softening with her normal teasing. "Let me help you over the ledge."

Liam exhaled slowly. They lifted on the count of three, effortlessly carrying it into the room.

Once the cart was steady she walked away without another word, and Liam pressed forward.

Virgil was by the window, watching the pod. Several of the creatures were hovering around his height, bobbing like dolphins as they kept up with the sub, alternating violet and blue.

He leaned forward, trying to peer around the corner of the sub. "I almost can't see the leader anymore."

Liam started taking objects off the cart. He pulled off the sheet, and then stared at the container, processing that they were about to do something against explicit commands.

46

"What did she want?" Virgil asked, almost whispering. His voice fogged the glass, turning it frosty.

"Nothing," Liam lied. "Just some friendly ribbing and then she was on her way. Shouldn't be a problem."

Virgil nodded, and Liam exhaled. But he had to force himself to let go of the fabric, and stared at the wrinkles he had made until he could see shapes in them.

"Liam," Virgil repeated, snapping him out of his daze. "Can you start the dive procedure?"

Liam nodded, dropping the fabric on the console on his way toward the decompression room.

The Dive Bay was built to let divers come and go while keeping water out. To do so, there were two sets of doors. The inner doors opened horizontally, like the automatic doors of a supermarket. Once divers were beyond those, the doors closed, and the room would slowly fill with water. Then the second door would open vertically, and the diver would be able to swim out into the sea.

Each diver had their own wetsuit, but there was only one dive suit. It looked like a retro scuba suit, with a large, circular fish bowl for a head, and an off-white, rubbery fabric for the body. When in use, the fabric filled with a thick fluid that helped the divers survive the deep-sea pressure, but at all other times it was flabby and loose.

Liam realized that, after days without a dive, this was the first time he had seen it dry. The thick fabric and rusted metal components had an odd sheen, and he forgot its rubbery, tire-like feel until he unhooked it from the wall.

Virgil set the canister on the ground beside him.

"You should..." Liam said, keeping his eyes on the wall and his voice calm and reasonable, "strip down. The fluid they use isn't good for clothes."

Virgil nodded, the expression on his face showing he hadn't considered this aspect.

"You can wear my wetsuit, if you'd like," Liam offered. "I think we're roughly the same size."

"Perhaps in height," Virgil said, chuckling, "but I fear it will be fairly loose on me everywhere else." Instead, he began unbuttoning his dress shirt, and Liam looked away and began fidgeting with the equipment. He heard a soft thud as Virgil's clothes were tossed into the corner. He glanced over at Virgil in his trunks. He looked determined, yet embarrassed, and he held his arms tight against his side to keep from shivering.

Liam swallowed the urge to hold him until he was warm again.

"Shall we get to work now?" Virgil asked, once again snapping Liam back to reality.

"Of course."

The suit was particular, with knobs and straps in unexpected places, but Liam could put it together in his sleep. Virgil strained visibly, suddenly carrying a hundred pounds of fabric and metal across his body, but he stayed upright. Liam fought between rushing to finish and making certain everything was secure. He lifted the fishbowl helmet and carefully set it over Virgil's head, then latched it.

"Are you sure you don't want a wetsuit?" Liam asked. "The cold is going to get to you pretty soon."

"If it doesn't fit, it won't help me anyway," he said.

Liam nodded. "Okay, but head back as soon as you start to feel any serious drop in temperature"

"Roger that. Would you mind handing me..." Virgil asked, gesturing to the container at his feet. "I can't exactly lean over."

Liam nodded. He set the tank into Virgil's outstretched arms, careful to make sure the container would be adequately cradled. "Alright. That should do it."

"Thank you," Virgil said.

"No problem."

"No. Thank you," Virgil repeated, his tone drawing Liam's attention. He was still wearing his glasses in the suit, so the double reflection created a unique glare. Liam could still see part of the brown peeking out from behind, though.

"For what?" Liam asked.

"For sticking your neck out like this," he said. "It means a lot to me. Well, to us."

Liam smiled weakly. "Well, don't thank me yet. I've got to get you back in safely first."

"I believe in you," he said

Liam looked away, suppressing the urge to smile. "Last step. Are you ready?"

"As I'll ever be," Virgil said.

Liam chuckled. "Okay. Heads up, it feels weird." He pressed a nearby button on the wall. The whir of machinery came alive as the slimy fluid that would keep Virgil's body pressure safe started to flow.

Virgil stiffened as the chilled liquid filled the suit. Instinctively, Liam grabbed the canister, supporting it from below and preventing it from slipping from Virgil's grip.

They stood for a moment, the air hissing as it was exhausted from the body of his suit. Virgil slid his hands under Liam's, the rough, rubbery texture of the gloves tickling as they slid across the back of his hand, reaching toward his wrist. Liam pulled away, worried Virgil might feel the increase in his pulse, but Virgil's grip tightened and Liam froze. He was sure he was blushing now from the heat in his cheeks.

The motor slowed to a halting buzz, and the suit was full. Virgil squeezed once more then let go, and Liam stepped away.

49

"You were right about the cold," Virgil said, finally. His voice was muffled through the helmet, and he fogged the glass while he spoke.

"We can stop," Liam offered.

"Too late for that," he said, somberly. His expression grew steely serious. "Any final notes for me? Before we finish this?"

Naida's voice teased from the back of Liam's mind. Nice things, and what they meant.

But there wasn't a single way Liam could think of saying what it meant to him that didn't feel like he was popping a bubble.

"You're going to do great," he said, finally.

A glare passed over the glass, making Virgil unreadable. "Then let's begin."

Liam hesitated, but nodded and exited the room. He took a deep breath, then pressed the button, closing the inner doors.

He ran to the control booth and scanned the instruments panel, flipping switches as the dive procedure began.

The lights flashed as water poured into the Dive Bay. From experience, he knew the weight of the suit would slowly lift from Virgil's shoulders as the water level rose. When the pressure increased, he would even begin to float.

Liam flipped a switch and he could hear Virgil's breathing through the communication equipment in his helmet. Another switch, and a group of TV screens turned on. Virgil was in the uppermost left screen, blurry under the rising water.

They waited for the room to fill, then a green light flashed on the console. Liam swallowed hard and pressed a button, leaning toward the microphone.

"I'm opening the door. Swim toward it when you're ready."

Ignoring the camera, Virgil stared ahead. The canister glowed with a diffused yellow light under his arm as he signaled for Liam to proceed. With another hard breath, Liam pressed the button, and the outer door stretched upward like a garage door.

Liam flipped on his mic again. "You're going to enter a blind spot at first, so try to get to the window as soon as possible."

"I'm going as quickly as I can. I'm not as strong a swimmer as you are," Virgil said.

"Not what I'd like to hear right now," Liam said, but after a minute the man floated in front of the window. He was being honest when he said he wasn't a strong swimmer; his already unsure movements were jerky and restricted in the suit. Liam giggled, despite himself. All vitals were green; they were good to go.

Virgil swam to the pod and righted himself. He pulled the canister from under his arm, staring at its contents. The light within changed from yellow to blue to green. He held a button, releasing the pressure inside, and slowly undid the latches with his gloved hands until it opened.

Theo peeked over the edge, glowing a cautious red, and pressed their fins flat against their body.

"Go on," Virgil said through his open mic. His voice was gentle, and an octave higher than normal. "You're safe." He reached toward the lip of the container, and Theo swam onto his hand like a bird perching on a finger.

Three members of the pod swooped down, each at least half the size of Virgil. They swam excitedly around the pair, their wake upsetting Virgil's balance until another swam up behind him and righted him mid-backspin.

"Oh my. Fascinating," Virgil said, following it with a cautious, "Thank you."

Theo's color changed to match theirs, and the group glowed a bright violet. Theo swam off Virgil's hand and darted from creature to creature like a puppy exploring a new room.

Theo swam against Virgil, sliding across the crook of his

neck. Virgil pet Theo for the first time, and they swam into his palm, nuzzling against the glove.

"I knew you'd like it here. I asked them to let you go as soon as we found the pod, but they wouldn't let me. They wanted to keep you for more study." Virgil said. There was a slight quiver in his voice, from cold or emotion or both. Liam glanced at his vitals and noticed his temperature dropping. The suit was cooling fast.

"Your vitals are dropping, Virgil," Liam said. "You need to head in."

"I know," Virgil said, his teeth chattering. "Just one moment."

Theo swam away and back again, beckoning Virgil forward.

Virgil chuckled. "No, I can't come with you. This is goodbye, I'm afraid."

Theo hovered in the water, their fins slowing to a somber wave, and Virgil reached out to pet them one last time. "We found you a family, Theo."

Theo pulsed with white light like they were shivering as well, but as the others swam around them, sweeping Theo up in their dance. The pod picked up speed, changing their course until they were perpendicular with the submarine.

"Take good care of them," Virgil said, as Theo was ushered away – the lights around them swirling like a somber song.

Liam glanced at the vitals. Ninety degrees Fahrenheit. They were well past the danger zone.

"Virgil, it's time to go," Liam said.

"I know, I know," he said, turning around. But his voice was quiet and slurred, his awkward swimming now lethargic. Liam gripped the dashboard, listening to the sound of teeth chattering through the mic. And then that began to slow as well.

"Virgil?" Liam said. No response. He watched Virgil float

52

into the camera's blind spot, panic welling in his throat.

He had to do something, but what? If he could, he would reel him in with the oxygen tube, but that could just as easily rip it out of the suit. He needed another way.

Liam's legs went weak, and he fought the urge to slide to the floor. His heartbeat was a ticking bomb, reverberating through his bones.

"Do something," he said to himself. "Do something."

On instinct, Liam reached across the control panel, closed the outer doors and then ran towards the Dive Bay. The decompression system started, draining water from the room. He had no visual on Virgil, so he had to estimate when he would pass by the outer doors. He counted the time in his head, then pressed the red override button, opening the outside doors mid-decompression.

The sudden change in pressure popped as gallons of water were sucked into the room, along with Virgil.

Liam pressed the button, closing the outers door once more. He watched on a screen as the water was removed. When he could no longer wait, he burst through the inner doors, stepping in the puddles left behind.

Virgil had rolled onto his back. Through the helmet, Liam saw his lips were blue.

Liam frantically undid the latches and straps. He lifted Virgil's torso up and laid him across his lap, the ice-cold liquid that filled the suit leaking through the seams and spilling onto his clothes.

"Virgil," Liam cried. "Virgil!"

Virgil moaned, coming back to consciousness. Liam ripped off the helmet, tossing it to the side. He rubbed Virgil's cheeks, trying to bring their color back.

"Virgil, are you–"

His gloved arm swung around Liam's neck and pulled him down. He had a moment to see Virgil's parted lips before they were upon his own, and then they were all he could feel. Virgil felt cold but tasted warm, like tea. He pulled Liam closer with a damp arm across his back. Seawater crept through the seat of Liam's pants but he hardly noticed as he melted into Virgil's arms.

Liam wasn't sure how long they kissed, but it wasn't long enough. When he pulled away, he noticed Virgil's cheeks were wet, too. He had been crying.

"I hope you don't mind," Virgil said. "I overheard a bit of your conversation with Ms. Naida."

"Not at all," Liam said. His heart was racing, but for once he didn't want it to settle down. He reached out to dry Virgil's cheek, but the action only invited more tears.

"Theo must have been so lonely," Virgil said, still shivering. Liam rubbed his neck and down his chest, kneading the warmth back into his skin. "Theo was all alone. When you found them."

"We didn't know, " Liam said, cautiously. He pulled Virgil's suit sleeve off, and grabbed his hand in both of his. "But I don't think Theo was lonely. They always had you."

Virgil reached up to dry his eyes, smearing the jelly substance on them and his glasses in the process.

"Thank you," Virgil said. "For saving my life."

"Anytime," Liam said. He helped Virgil to his feet, and led him towards the warm showers around the corner.

"Perhaps," Virgil started, "I should stick to simpler pets."

EVVAN BURKE is a UCSD graduate in Critical Gender Studies and Writing. His work can be found crawling out of the graveyard of print media. He can occasionally be found on Phaserburn. tumblr.com, and @Phaserburn on Instagram and Twitter.

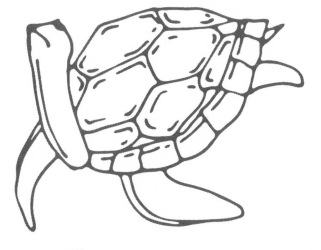

THE SELKIE WIFE

by Lia Cooper

After four hundred years, you develop more than just a rhythm.

Marion Wylde sat reading on the shores of the Roanoke River while the late summer sun crawled slowly across the sky. Every year civilization crept a little bit closer to her doorstep, but here, tucked away in this one bend in the river, she could still enjoy her afternoon without the sound of cars growling down US Route 460 on their way to Salem.

She read and waited for Sybil to return, to catch a glimpse of her dark head breaking the water, for her little seal-wife to emerge, grinning and shaking off her wet skin like she did every seven years. Seven years they lived together in the hag's cottage by the river – a real cottage now with a kitchen and a bedroom and a greenhouse for growing herbs during the winter, a far cry from the rough-cut log cabin she'd built herself by hand. And seven years they lived apart while Sybil returned to her pod in the deep cold dark Atlantic. A fair trade in Marion's book.

So, she waited, she read, she baked bread, and put up flowers to dry under the eaves. And in the evenings she sat out until the sun went down, with one eye trained on the softly burbling stream.

Any day now.

And as the centuries passed, the oceans warmed, the ice caps melted, and the ocean swelled.

Sybil dozed in the cool waters off the Newfoundland coast. Her dark brown eyes slipped closed while a part of her brain kept right on clicking away, tuned to the electrical currents in the water, as though a third eye remained trained on the ocean depths, tensed for any sign of predators or prey.

This late in the summer, as she began her migration away from her pod's native shores, Sybil was loathe to pass up any chance at choice fish. Her body still carried the weight she'd packed onto her bones through spring and early summer, thick blubber that would see her through her journey, even though pickings grew slim the further south she traveled.

The world shrank, faster every year it seemed, as the boats – those great sailing beasts that had once taken months to traverse the treacherous Atlantic – now crisscrossed the globe faster than she could ever hope to follow. They hauled up the bounty of the ocean while she and her kin struggled every year to gorge themselves enough before winter.

Once, the shores off Montauk and Hatteras had teemed with fish enough to feed a hundred pods and never run dry. But that had been an age ago.

As her body sank slowly under the gray-blue, Sybil twitched herself awake. A few powerful kicks of her back flippers propelled her to the surface where her dark gray-brown snout breached, sucking in crisp air. She slid sideways through the water another hundred yards, tacking with the winds of the Labrador Current, before she let her body relax into the soft swell of the water.

She traveled on the schedule ingrained in her senses, not in any great hurry just yet. Seven years she'd swum with her pod, and by the end of the season she'd be back with her hag-wife on the shores of a little river – nothing more than a trickle to a selkie used to the wide ocean – where she'd live off bread and rabbit meat for another seven years.

Her mouth watered at the thought of rabbit roasted in its own fats, green beans, and potatoes – all of those land foods Marion knew she loved and never ate at sea. Oh, to swim up that little trickle again and shed her seal-skin for a little while.

When her half-sleeping body began to sink again, Sybil roused herself, but this time she turned and dove, stretching out her senses in the cool dark for a sign of something to eat. Just one more morsel, one more fish gobbled up whole, she told herself. Something sleek and bloody to quench her thirst and carry her through the night and the morrow's journey.

She could sense a thin shoal of North Atlantic cod zipping through the water one hundred feet down, just above the ocean floor. Their bodies sent tiny ripples through the water, both physical and electromagnetic, that helped Sybil zero in on their location and direction. She dove, dark eyes fixed on the black as it rushed up to meet her, and imagined Marion's hearth waiting for her.

It was a selkie-maid's fate to be captured once in her life. Every young cow was caught eventually, her skin stolen away by some greedy fisherman for seven years. Sybil had been caught, fished out of a shallow stream she should not have wandered into, and kept by a curious hag-wife for seven years. They'd lived just the two of them in the dusky-blue mountains of a wild, empty land, never seeing hide nor hair of another in all that time. And when the first seven years were over, the hag had brought out

Sybil's seal-skin, wrapped it around her wife's shoulders, and helped her slip back into that stream with one final kiss bussed across her damp black nose.

It was a selkie-maid's fate to be captured once; it was not in her nature to be caught a second time. Or a third.

For seven years after she returned to her pod, Sybil had swum deep and fast, lived off salty fish again, and brushed off the advances of the bulls who would have taken her to be their sea-wives. Her disinterest in their advances hadn't been seen as anything more than youthful disinterest until she'd followed the current south again, followed her nose to that same little inland stream back to a little log cottage tucked away in half-remembered mountains.

For seven years she had walked on two feet and slept in Marion's bed until the call of the sea drew her away, but she could never stay permanently away. Before too long, and without fail, her flippers propelled her back again.

Lost in daydreams, Sybil dove into the shoal. The fish were small, barely two feet in length, juveniles who slithered and split around her as she looped through them. Their slick, silver bodies shivered against her in terror as she snapped her teeth into a tender side, jaws locked tight around a young cod's body, the taste of its blood bursting quick and bright on her thick tongue.

She didn't realize her mistake until she turned to climb for the surface and her nose pressed into the fine, nearly translucent line.

Four hundred years ago, a single woman didn't come to the New World on her own; she came as a colonist's wife. At least, that's how it had been when Marion sailed across the wild Atlantic with her short-lived husband.

For more than four hundred years, Marion Wylde had been living in her little cottage along the Roanoke River, and she couldn't have recalled his countenance if you'd stuck a shotgun in her face. She'd married him because it had been the only way to escape the tiny English village that would have burned her as a witch, given another year or two. Married and buried him within the first year of the colony.

There was only so much one woman could do to keep a hundred Englishmen alive when they seemed dead set on perishing from malnutrition and foolishness.

She left the remains of the colony after that first winter, wandering inland, following the river and trading for a little canoe that carried her all the way to the mountains. She was a hag, her mother's mother's last surviving girl, and what was thirty years spent wandering to a woman like her?

Marion built herself a little house on the river, tucked deep in the forest. She kept to herself, occasionally traded with one of the people of the river, grew a garden, trapped rabbits for their fur and meat, and spent many days sitting by the stream with a slender fishing rod in her hand.

Having escaped the threat of civilization, she expected to live out the rest of her very long life in a similar, solitary way. She never planned to fish up a seal-wife on the shores of her little cabin, but these things happen from time to time.

Sybil nosed against the fine mesh, the fish in her jaws thrashing weakly in its death throes. She bit and swallowed a hunk of flesh and blood before letting the rest slip from her surprised mouth. Her back flippers churned as she pressed herself carefully against the netting, traced the edges while the panicked cod turned and flicked in an increasingly narrow corridor of water.

Below them, the ocean bed kicked up pale dust and rock where the weights on the netting dug furrows into the sand. She felt her body carried along with the shoal as it was herded by the movement of the net.

She tried to kick herself ahead of the fish, but the grit and scales obscured her vision. She could stay underwater for a dozen minutes or more without trouble, so she didn't panic at first. This was not the first net that Sybil had ever encountered in her long life.

There was something electric in the ambiance of the water around her, however, a kind of fish-knowledge rippled through the shoal as they were dragged towards the surface. Sybil twisted around thrice as she oriented herself up and forward, snapping her mouth at unwary cod as she cut a path through them, lungs straining and eyes burning against the commotion as she sought the mouth of the net.

Oh, for a pair of her human hands and one of those clever knives they used! She could have sliced her way out of this mess as smoothly as Marion cut into the belly of her meals.

Sybil made a high-pitched squeal that rippled through the cod, sent them buzzing out of her way as she thrashed along the wall of the net. All she had to do was find the opening before it closed or before the catch was hauled out of the ocean. The trawlers weren't out there for seal flesh and oil, but that rarely mattered. A profit was a profit, and Sybil had no intention of her seal-skin being turned into the collar of a Dior runway coat.

The haul rapidly approached the surface; Sybil could feel it as her body adjusted to the changes in temperature and water pressure. She double backed as the mouth of the net drew tight, flattening with the drag from the stinking lead weights. Her back fins spun, propelling her forward in a rush as she nosed her way into the gap, slipping free in the lighter water. The bottom of the fishing boat eclipsed the whole sky, a huge dark blur above her. She swam under and past the boat, kept swimming until her lungs burned and she could safely breach, out of range of any ambitious harpoons.

Sybil bobbed in the Atlantic, smacking her lips against the salty air. Her eyes were better underwater, but she could still make out the dim figures of the men as they worked to swing the writhing net over the side of their boat, disgorging the adolescent cod onto the deck. She watched for some time, waiting for her hammering heart to slow, and then she spun and ducked under the waves, headed south again. She sought out the swift-moving current that would carry her all the way down to Hatteras, ducking up for air before slipping below the surface again and again, beating her back fins against the sea.

The end of summer couldn't come quickly enough, she decided, thinking of Marion's dry bed and the smell of herbs in the air to tickle her nose.

It was a shock, that hot afternoon when Marion's hook caught in the flipper of a honking, speckled seal. She barely had a word for the beast, having seen no such creature in the New World, and only glimpses of the small speckled seals that sunned themselves on the rocky shores of her native England. The animal thrashed against the edge of the stream and flicked its flipper hard enough to jerk her willow rod right out of her hands. Marion had cursed and splashed into the stream after it, wrestling with the seal until she was soaked through to her skin, triumphant with the hooked fly in hand. Metal was too precious for her to lose a piece in such a way.

She'd waded out of the Roanoke River, shivering as the sun began to set, and picked up her rod to carry it back to the cottage when she heard a tremendous splash and the slap of feet following her up the bank.

"Is that all, then?" a sharp voice demanded, so high and rusty and full-throated, it shivered down her spine and left her ears tingling.

Marion turned and clapped eyes on a young woman, fish-pale and naked with long dark hair, small pert breasts, and peaked nipples, all of her dripping water. A dark bundle in her hand trailed into the rushing water.

Marion gaped at the strange woman, speechless. She hadn't spoken to another living soul, leastwise not a human one, in several years and as she stared, mouth flapping in surprise, she wondered if she'd forgotten how.

The woman shook her head like an animal shaking water off its back and stepped carefully up the bank, picking her knees up high as though she were afraid of falling – as though she were unused to walking. The dark bundle in her hands came trailing along after her until she bent to gather it up into her arms, careful of the mud. When she was done, she straightened and looked at Marion expectantly, holding out the bundle to her with an impatient noise.

"Well?"

Marion shook her head and reached automatically to take the offering, but stopped herself. She frowned.

"What?" Marion asked, surprised at the sound of her own rough voice. "Where did you come from?"

"The river, of course."

"I beg pardon?"

The strange woman crowded into her personal space, pressing the bundle – some kind of thick animal skin, soft and silky – into her hands until she was forced to take it.

"You may call me Sybil," the woman said. "And what should

64

I call you?"

"How did you come from the river?"

Sybil cocked her head to one side with a frown. "The usual way." She gestured back over her shoulder, downriver toward where it wound its way out of the mountains and all the way to the sea. She grabbed Marion by her elbows, squeezing tight. "But what should I call you, wife?"

"Pardon?" Marion repeated, her voice failing her as Sybil stood up on tiptoe – half a head shorter, with the two of them barefoot on the shore. The strange woman's hair trailed cold against Marion's cheek as she brought their faces together, brushed her mouth against Marion's in the first kiss she'd received since her wedding day.

When Sybil pulled away, she smiled curiously, head still cocked askew as she stepped around Marion and headed to the cottage.

"I don't suppose you caught any fish while you were at it? I'm starving," she called over her shoulder.

Marion rushed to catch up, hands full of seal-skin.

Now, Marion closed her book with a sigh and stared downstream, but all she could see were the late summer trees bending over the swift flowing banks of the river as it disappeared from view. She gathered her things and headed back to the house.

Marion had held off modernizing her corner of the forest for years, unwilling to create an identity for herself that could pay electric bills, but she'd finally installed a little solar panel on the roof. It stored just enough energy during the day to power a couple of appliances as well as a small refrigerator. Sybil had developed a taste for ice cream over the last century, and Marion couldn't wait to see the look on her face when she saw the stock of sweet creams she'd laid down in the freezer.

It was the last day of August when she propped open the cottage door, the screen in place to keep out the mosquitoes on that hot night. She trailed her hand over the side of the humming refrigerator and sighed.

Any day now, she reminded herself.

For more than four hundred years they'd been doing this, even though it wasn't entirely natural for a selkie. It had nearly broken her heart to give up Sybil's seal-skin after those first seven years together, but she'd done it, knowing that she'd never see her little selkie-wife again. Marion had lived those first seven years apart trying to forget what it meant to sleep beside another warm body in her bed, to be mocked every time she took her willow rod down to the river, to have a set of hands to steal around her waist when she stood at the kitchen work table preparing meals.

Marion knew how lucky she was that Sybil had come back... that she kept coming back.

"Any day now," she murmured to the dark and felt her heart ache with the worry that always came late in the seventh summer: maybe this would be the time her selkie-wife stayed lost at sea.

Somewhere off the southern coast of New England, Sybil drifted on her back in the early morning light, enjoying the way the waters buoyed her body while she slurped lobster meat out of the cracked shells. Below her, a dozen lobster pots cut a line from the dock, mostly empty, and emptier still after her bit of breakfast thievery.

When she had finished her meal, she turned herself a couple of times in the water, splashing the stink off her muzzle. She bobbed there, watching the shore drift by at a lazy pace while her stomach digested.

She'd made good time since her brush with the cod trawler, but it was hard to tell just how far she had left to travel in this form. She didn't navigate as a seal the same way she would as a woman. At sea, she had the gentle tug and pull of the earth's electromagnetic sphere to safely carry her across the large expanse of ocean, and her nose to guide her up the correct stream. But on land, all she had were her eyes and an unreliable human intuition, one that had led her astray more often than not. Where to turn right and where to turn left if every concrete road looks the same?

For all the time they'd spent living in their little corner of the world, it seemed like Sybil became lost the second she left it on two feet. The trees and mountains looked the same, and she didn't find the recent advent of street signs to be any more clear. She'd never much taken to reading herself; why would she need to when she had Marion to read to her?

So when she oriented herself by the sun and the current, propelling her sleek, fat seal-body through the water, she kept her eyes at half-mast, trained to watch for predators rather than landmarks, and let her nose do the work of finding the right place to turn inland.

The summer slipped away as she traversed the Atlantic. She wasn't in the habit of counting days in this form, so she didn't grow concerned about her progress until the days began to grow noticeably shorter.

Sybil moved toward the shore, letting the current do most of the work while she scanned the long strip of land. She looked for anything familiar, her nose sifting through the cloying scents that grew stronger as the land grew larger.

As the world had shrunk around Sybil and Marion, as the population of ordinary people exploded, the stench of industry had grown until Sybil thought it was all she'd smell anymore: oil and gas, engine runoff that pooled in greasy slicks outside harbors, garbage and sewage, smog on the air. She hated swimming through the bigger port cities. They'd traveled to New York once, to see all the ways it had sprung up since the Dutch first settled there three hundred years ago. The smells – well, Sybil had never smelled anything quite so rank as that, and she tried to swim well clear of it each year during her migration.

Now, she bobbed on the dirty water of a nameless harbor and watched the big shipping liners sail in and out all afternoon.

Every stream and estuary had a unique scent, a certain combination of artificial contaminants and the waterway's natural makeup that keyed into her seal-brain how far she'd traveled. Sybil should have reached her own little stream already, but her head felt all muddled in the dying light; the water too warm, the dust on the air too thick and burnt, not quite like anything she could remember. So she swam closer to shore, past the big harbor with the mammoth commercial liners, to a strip of beach.

There she paddled around the shallows, one eye trained on the beach. But humans tended to all look the same to Sybil, especially when she was in her seal-body.

A roar overtook her ears, building above the noise of the waves rolling in – the whine of some high-pitched, motorized engine. Sybil's head swiveled in a sharp arc as she spun in the water, trying to orient herself. She dove as it roared over her, heart thundering as fast as the water swirling in the jet ski's wake.

Sybil dove deep, deeper than she needed to be safe, until the soft, sandy ocean floor came into view. She spun and watched the dark, slender vehicle cut a path across the surface until the roar finally faded away. Then she swam toward shore, staying low in the water as long as her lungs allowed before surfacing to breathe and dive again. She followed a rocky outcropping to a more secluded part of the beach and only climbed out when the daylight slipped away, leaving her shrouded in careful night.

She hauled herself out onto a rock, panting and shivering in the dark, not from the cold but from the way her little seal-heart beat too fast in her breast. She found a niche in the rock and curled herself up tight, one eye open to watch the stars as they winked on above her.

Sybil dozed for an hour or two until the last clouds melted away to reveal a dark, brilliant sky. The low light pollution here was lighter than she could have hoped for as she mapped familiar constellations. She found the edge of the hungry bear fishing in the river, the clever old salmon as he leapt the stream to safety, and bled into the tail of the great white whale waiting to devour him. She stared until her eyes burned.

Finally, her heart settled as she oriented herself to these constellations. No matter how small the world grew, no matter how warm the oceans boiled, or how the refuse polluted the once-familiar scents of her migration, humanity hadn't found a way to change the map of the stars.

Not yet.

August bled into a hot, sticky September when Marion drove in to buy a copy of the local paper. It wasn't a usual routine for her, but they printed the fifteen-day forecast on Sundays, and Marion sat on the tailgate of her truck, scanning the National section for any hurricane news. She kicked her heels in the air, chin propped on her knee while she worried at a hole in her jeans and scanned the newsprint, but there was nothing exciting to read there. Only a long-winded opinion in the editorial section about the Atlantic Coast Pipeline.

They'd halted construction on it up north when a sinkhole

opened up beneath a section of the six-hundred-mile pipe in North Carolina.

"Environmental experts project that the pipeline will have the same effect on the region as twenty coal-fired power plants. This did not stop Domino Energy, CGLM from beginning construction on the project early last year..."

When she drove home that evening, she stared at the dark, reflective surface of the lake, nails digging into the steering wheel until she'd left ten perfect indentations in the worn pleather. She climbed out of the truck and slammed the door, single key spinning on her keyring as she walked up the overgrown path to her front door. The Roanoke trickled by with a soft, unbroken burble that made Marion's heart feel tight and heavy in her chest. She opened the door and slipped in a puddle of water on the threshold.

Her heart only beat again once she flicked on the small string of fairy lights illuminating half the cottage. Dark, smeared footsteps led into the bedroom; she followed them, shucking off her crocs and tearing off her dusty clothes until she finally caught a glimpse of fish-pale skin sprawled across the bed, dark hair trailing off the edge in a matted curtain.

When Sybil looked up, she had a pinched, drawn expression on her face. It crumpled as Marion crossed the room. The selkie held out her cool arms, welcoming Marion into them as a little noise wrenched out of her throat.

"Oh," Sybil whispered, wrapping her limbs around Marion tighter than an octopus. "Oh, I couldn't find the right stream. Everything smelled hot and awful. Like that dumpster behind Patty's Diner. I had to follow the stars and it took so much longer than I planned."

Marion caught a flash of dark seal-skin hanging over the windowsill. She plucked a bit of tangled plastic out of Sybil's hair

70

and tossed it onto the bare plank floor.

"That's alright," she murmured, pressing soft closed-mouth kisses against the selkie's skin. "I think you're allowed to be late once in four hundred years."

LIA COOPER is a twenty-something native of the Pacific Northwest, reader, and pop-culture addict. She won NaNoWriMo in 2012, and has dabbled in professional catering, barista-ing, and working as a pastry chef before finally returning to storytelling. Follow her on her blog liacooper.com, Twitter @LiaCooperWrites, and YouTube at youtube.com/c/LiaCooper.

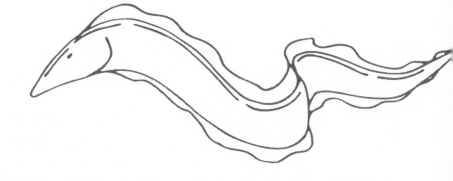

STUCK

by Mharie West

"And here come the happy couple, the Princess of Old Wales arm-in-arm with Mariana, her soon-to-be wife."

Lian stared blankly at the small, bad-quality television and let the deep-voiced commentator drone on, saying things everyone listening would already know. Mariana would be styled the Duchess of Cornwall... she and Princess Anne had been engaged for four years... Anne was the heir-apparent to the throne of Great Britain... Queen Anne III...

She winced hard as the commentator deadnamed Mariana. Someone needed to check who that AI had been interacting with as it wrote its lines.

The signal flickered again, casting a brief strobe effect over the tiny kitchen area. *Oh, come on.* Even ten miles underwater and relying on an uplink from a station the next planet over, she expected better than this. The TV signal in their little underwater habitat ("hab") was generally excellent.

Why are you watching TV anyway? she asked herself. *It's not helping.*

She told that particular thought what it could go and do, and carried on wallowing in other people's romance and happiness. Like quicksand, the more she tried to move on with life, the further she sank into the depths of despair.

Everything reminded her of Clare. If she walked into a door, Clare's mockery would hang in the air, and stars forbid Lian find any of Clare's clothes mixed in with hers. Why was that still *happening?* Lian only had a week's worth of clothes with her!

The problem wasn't that Clare was gone – okay, not *entirely* that – it was that she had gone without a word. Lian had come back from her first underwater moon deployment and most of Clare's stuff was gone.

It had taken her several frantic days before the facts were laid bare: Clare had left their home together and gone back to Mars and had refused to accept her messages or calls since.

The disaster had happened the day before her twentieth solar birthday, four months ago. On impulse, Lian had signed straight back up to another planetary ocean contract and so, here she was. Miles underwater on the Saturnian moon of Mimas in a tiny fragile little habitat, trying to build up a picture of the food web for their assigned area.

She should have been over the dumping by now, but instead she had just got more angry and upset. It was the lack of an explanation she couldn't handle. There was a hole in her life and Clare had given her no reason for it.

"You look like you're having fun." Her hab-mate and fellow scientist Quilet came into the kitchen, nir black and white galaxy-patterned hair bound up in a silk scarf to protect it from the chemicals of the quick-shower. Said chemicals usually played havoc with Lian's skin, but Quilet's skin was glistening like amber.

Lian reluctantly went along with Quilet's distraction to drag herself out of her personal quicksand.

"So much fun, thanks Quilet. I can recite the queen's lineage all the way back to Earth, want to hear?"

Quilet pulled a face. "I'd rather go back outside," ne said, and waved a freckled hand aimlessly at the walls.

They didn't have windows. Who would want to see inky blackness day in and day out? Hab designers had eventually realized deep-sea windows were a bad idea.

Lian watched listlessly as Quilet made nirself breakfast. Ne was absolutely gorgeous, and flirtatious when ne wanted to be, but Lian didn't think she should try to stuff someone into the Clare-hole while it was still raw.

She was sure Quilet was looking for something uncomplicated. Lian came with extra helpings of complicated.

Nevertheless, she felt heat rise to her face as Quilet shook her shoulder. Nir hand was warm and it made her skin tingle pleasantly.

"Mimas to Lian? Are you going outside, or am I *actually* pulling a double shift for you?"

"Okay." Lian stood up and sighed. "Okay."

The dry suit felt clammy against Lian's skin as she pulled it on and ran through the safety checks at top speed. She ignored it. She was late already – hab scraping with only two people was a constant battle and she really should have been standing next to the airlock when Quilet came back in. She'd check the dry suit over when she got back inside.

The floating blackness of the sea engulfed her. For a long moment she relaxed into the peace of it and let the gentle current push her around.

She didn't have the luxury of relaxing, she chided herself. She had a job to do.

She flicked on the blazing white headlamp and the blackness came to life.

Thousands upon thousands of xenoplankton used the hab as their resting place. They were too small to see, but they were chased by larger, many-legged creatures perhaps the size of Lian's thumb, which were translucent and colorless, as expected miles away from sunlight.

She turned around in the water to face the hab. She and Quilet had been living there for three months now, but looking at the structure which was keeping them alive still made Lian's spine tingle.

It was made up of four clumped-together spheres. One for the kitchen, one for the bedroom, one for the bathroom, and one for the entrance and exit, which kept the water out of everywhere else. The spheres were all lashed down tightly onto the ocean floor with top-quality high-tension material, but the hab still shifted in the ocean basin current. Good sea-legs were essential.

She swam around it until she could see where Quilet had stopped scraping. It was a stark contrast: bare hab against fuzzy masses of red algae growths.

Lian stared at the amount of work ne had done in disbelief. Had Quilet found a soft patch or something? She drew out the long-handled metal scraper and shook it open. Unfolded, the blade was several times wider than she was. Tentatively she poked at the algae next to Quilet's patch. Nope, sure enough, only a few red flecks drifted away. Quilet had done a *really* good job today.

Lian felt her will dip at the very thought of the work ahead of her, but she gritted her teeth and hefted her scraper.

The spade-like blade sank into the algae. Feeling the resistance that meant she had hit a root colony, she twisted the blade upwards and pulled. A clump three times as wide as she was peeled off, leaving almost completely bare hab underneath.

Well, that had been satisfying, Lian admitted, but it had also been a bit like spitting into a volcano. She sighed and set her alarm for the end of shift.

"Lian! Lian, answer me!"

She blinked. "Hi, Quilet." Her thoughts were slow and fuzzy and the scraper was pointing loosely at her feet. There was a loud ringing sound. Was that the phone?

"Lian! I've called you like six times! You should be back by now! Are you okay?"

She rolled the scraper from side to side in her hands and watched the xenoplankton-eaters wriggle to and fro in her headlamp beam. It looked like an old video she'd seen recently of someone kicking an ant's nest.

Her side was itchy. She tried to scratch it through the suit but the material was too thick. Eventually she replayed Quilet's words and realized ne had asked a question.

"I'm okay."

"Are you still outside the hab?"

Lian bristled at the sharp tone in nir voice. "Yeah, of course." But then she looked around and all she could see everywhere was black and the dancing, dancing little bugs eating away. "Quil?" Her voice squeaked.

"I'm coming out. Try and stay where you are." Nir voice was calm and steady now.

Lian was coherent enough to realize she wasn't thinking properly, which wasn't helpful; it just made her scared. The loud ringing noise she could hear wasn't the phone after all. It was her alarm. How long had she been out here for?

"Quil?" she wailed.

"I'm on my way. It's okay, sweetheart."

Normally Lian would roll her eyes at the endearment, but right now it was very welcome. "Talk to me," she begged. She tried to scratch her side again, unsuccessfully.

"Okay, so, I watched the rest of your wedding video. Mariana has similar hair to yours, all red and silver. It's nice. Uh, we've run out of oil for the spin-fryer – can't make you any more *accras* until we surface..." Ne chattered on; Lian tried to focus but nir voice kept receding into a comforting hum.

She came back to awareness with a terrifying jolt as something yanked her tether. There were no big aquatic predators here, but she still screamed and tugged back as hard as she could.

"It's me, Lian. It's only me. You'd drifted away." A gentler tug. "Pulling you back now, okay, babes?"

She had a vague sense of Quilet holding her tightly, which made her itchy side suddenly hurt, and then nothing.

When Lian next opened her eyes and paid attention to the world, it felt like she'd been out of it for a while. She was lying in bed. Her side still hurt. She poked it gingerly, then lifted the duvet and her top with clumsy fingers. Her abdomen was wrapped in bandages. The sight of it made her stomach flip. The wound was... big. Really big.

The last few moments before she passed out played back in her memory – jerky and uncertain, like the worst TV signal ever. Confusion, pain, and a long time outside clearing algae...

She grabbed the loose bandage end and unwrapped it. It wasn't her best decision, but it was one she felt she had to make. She needed to see.

The ragged red and yellow hole in her side stretched from her hip to the bottom of her ribcage. It was shallow, but messy and glistening. Her stomach flipped again.

"Oh come on, darling, do you know how long that takes to wrap? I only changed it two hours ago!" Quilet came in and sat gently on the bed next to her. Too gently – normally ne'd bounce

78

down hard.

"I'm fine," she blurted out.

"Uh-huh." Quilet's dark eyes were soft but nir face was stern. "That's why you're staring at that mess and looking like you're about to hurl."

Lian looked at it again. Shuddered. Her hab-mate settled closer to Lian until their bodies were resting together all up one side.

"The vampire algae?" she asked, knowing she was right even as she hoped she wasn't. Quilet nodded and Lian swore under her breath. The tiny carnivorous creatures stunned and dissolved their victims. They were the main danger of being out in the water, but since they couldn't dissolve their way through the outer layer of their specialist dry suits, the divers were usually... fine...

Dry suit.

Hers had been clammy. Damp.

She had raced through the checks, paying them minimal attention, completely on autopilot.

Wet dry suit meant perforated dry suit. One of the key safety lessons and she'd just ignored it.

I could have died, she thought. The words felt like stones. *They could have eaten further in and killed me and Quilet would have dragged in a corpse.*

A full-body shudder gripped her.

All because I wouldn't stop moping. The thought rattled around her head.

Quilet patted her knee.

"Alright?"

Lian fumbled for something to say. "Never been so thankful I'm fat." Well... unorthodox, but truthful. If she'd been thinner, there might have been damage to her organs.

Quilet jogged her very gently in the ribs. "Maybe now you'll appreciate it."

"Why? You appreciate it enough for both of us," Lian replied. Her brain chased the comment to its full conclusion and presented to her the suddenly embarrassing fact that she was wearing nightclothes.

Quilet had seen her naked.

Her skin was a few shades darker than Quilet's, and for the thousandth time in her life she thanked the genetic fluke that rendered her blushing almost invisible.

"I suppose you got an eyeful, then?" Her mouth spoke without her brain's interference, and she wanted the bed to swallow her up.

Quilet sat up a little and took nir hand off Lian's knee. It opened a gap between their bodies and the cooler air made her skin tingle.

"Well, I mean, I wasn't actually thinking about it when I was trying to get the skin-dissolving shitheads off you." Quilet's face was slightly reproachful. Ne spoiled the effect almost immediately by grinning and adding, "Do you want me to think about it now?"

Lian laughed, getting even hotter with embarrassment, and buried her head in the pillow. "*Qui–il...*"

Ne settled back against her. "Okay. Maybe we should have this conversation when you're less poisoned."

"I'm fine," Lian mumbled, and fell asleep as soon as she'd finished.

When she next opened her eyes, Quilet was gone. Probably to scrape. Lian stared at the curved ceiling for a while.

She wasn't upset anymore. It was the strangest feeling. She could still remember how she had felt scant hours before, sucked down into a neverending apathetic vortex of misery, but now

80

there was a barrier stopping her descent. She almost felt light and free. Even poking at the thought of Clare like a rotten tooth just made her wistful.

So what if someone who hadn't spoken to her in four months never spoke to her again? What did that matter, when she could have died today? She suddenly, desperately didn't want to waste the rest of her life pining, being this selfish, thoughtless, energy-sap of a person.

She thought of Quilet. Flirty, gorgeous Quilet, who had saved her life and looked after her Who liked her hair and her body and was such a lovely person. Ne deserved better than who Lian had been recently.

Lian could do better. She *would*.

Two days later, Quilet alerted the home base about the algae attack.

Lian saw red.

"Why did you do that?" she shouted at Quilet. "I'm fine now!"

"Oh, shut up!" Quilet shouted back. They stood in the tiny kitchen, glaring at each other over the counter. "If you were *fine*, you'd remember the *rules*!" Quilet slapped the counter for emphasis.

"I know the rules!" Lian stormed off – as best as she could in the confined space.

She paced around their shared bedroom until she stopped flushing hot with anger every time she thought about the argument, then sighed and sat down on her bed.

She *did* know the rules. Quilet had been absolutely right.

A vampire algae infestation always prompted medical evacuation up to the civ – the nearest "civilization" base with full facilities – for a full check-up, and often a complete scouring of the hab as well. Their little pile of bubbles wouldn't be habitable again for six months.

But more importantly to Lian, an evacuation also meant a full report to the director about how she had ended up in that situation, and she couldn't think up a plausible lie that didn't make her sound incompetent. Even the truth was embarrassing: "I let my personal problems distract me to the point that I didn't do basic safety checks."

She was halfway through a projected conversation involving her being fired on the spot when Quilet poked nir head in the door.

"You've been in here a while," ne said, nir tone carefully neutral.

Lian shrugged but said nothing. The panic from her imagined conservation was making her throat tight.

This was what got you into this, she scolded herself, *being too stuck in your own head.*

"Hey."

She blinked and looked up at Quilet. Ne sighed and bounced onto the bed next to Lian, and she could suddenly hear her own heartbeat. "Did you miss me already?"

"Always." Quilet grinned, but unexpectedly ne reached out and squeezed Lian's hand. "Keep in touch once we're land-side again, yeah?"

Lian's face felt like it was on fire. "I–Yeah. That would be great, yeah!" *Seize your chances*, she told herself. "We can go grab some food or something." She swallowed. "As a date."

Quilet gave a strange little laugh. "You can take back that offer when you're less algae-addled if you want, but I'd like that." As if ne could hear Lian's protesting thoughts, ne lifted their linked hands and, as a reminder, showed Lian the hives that had spread over most of her body.

They were so close they were basically hugging. Everywhere they were touching felt hot and over-sensitive and lovely.

"Okay, fine," Lian mumbled, and tried not to stare too hard at Quilet's lips.

Two months later, back on the civ, Lian waved nervously as she spotted Quilet hovering in the restaurant doorway. Nir hair was silver and spiky now as opposed to the swirling star patterns Lian had got used to, and as ne approached, Lian saw that ne'd had full eye tattooing done as well – nir eyes were solid black. It was a stunning change from their previous soft green.

"Pretty," she said, kicking out a chair from the long bar for Quilet. Ne mock-bowed and sat down, blocking Lian's view of how amazing nir calves looked in the long-sleeved leotard ne was wearing. "Your eyes are stunning," she said.

"Homage to the deep; I said I'd get it done after my first underwater stint. Never thought about getting anything yourself? Whale fin on your face? Seaweed along your arm?"

"Conservative parents, remember?" Which was true, but she had also never had anything permanent enough in her life and didn't think she should start with body modification.

Lian fiddled with the holographic menu, though she'd already picked her order and Quilet probably had too – ne had sung praises of the authenticity of this Guadeloupean cuisine bar many times at the hab – but they both awkwardly busied themselves staring at the 3D food representations.

Lian poked the e-waiter.

"Good evening, humans, may I take your order?"

She ordered *accras* and Quilet ordered *blaff*.

"And two *ti-punch*," Quilet added.

"Quil!" But she grinned even as she tried to sound outraged. They were firmly ashore and on a date. Why not have a bit to drink?

The alcohol smoothed out their conversation, and they recaptured the easy chat and banter they had developed undersea. Which meant, more flirting, more wriggling closer and closer in their chairs.

Several drinks later, Lian reached for Quilet's hair, only just stopping herself in time.

"Sorry. Uh, can I?" She gestured.

"Sure." Quilet leaned in. Nir hair was still soft despite the spikes. More importantly, they were now very close to each other. Lian could see herself faintly reflected in Quilet's augmented eyes.

To hell with it, she thought, and leaned in for the kiss.

Quilet surged in like a wave. One hand cupped Lian's face and the other went to the back of her neck. Lian's hand squeezed tight in Quilet's hair while her other hand flopped around uncertainly.

Their lips meshing in a warm and dry embrace, Lian was briefly struck by the thought that this wasn't how Clare kissed, which she fought down hard.

She parted her lips and let the present obliterate the past.

She shivered and bit Quilet's lip as ne moved from holding her face to stroking her side. Surfacing from a long underwater stint always made her skin incredibly sensitive. Normally she hated that side-effect but right now it was magnifying everything tenfold.

A loud *clank* from the kitchen startled them apart. She stared at Quilet's flushed face. Her body itched with the need for skin-to-skin contact, but they were in separate chairs, not to mention *in public*.

She wanted to lick Quilet's collarbone.

"Why didn't we start doing this when we were underwater?" she mumbled.

Quilet poked her ample abdomen. "That was definitely *your* fault. Let's go." Ne stood up. "You can make it up to me."

Lian got to her feet, a touch unsteadily, and cupped Quilet's cheek in her hand. "That'll take a while."

MHARIE WEST learned how to read a book with one hand so she could read while brushing her teeth, eating, showering, and so on... Writing seemed like the next step. Mharie loves worldbuilding and occasionally manages to put words on the page too, generally in the fantasy and historical fiction genres. She tweets at @WestMaz. Love & Bubbles is her first publication.

A HAPPY PLACE

by Maggie Derrick

Whistler's Bay was ten thousand residents small and the cutest town Nixie Wells had ever seen.

She hated it anyway.

As the Golden Coast Express pulled into its final stop on the line, she glared out her cabin window at the place of her exile.

It didn't matter that its whimsical little houses were filled with happy, hardworking people, or that the town itself was said to be nestled along the prettiest stretch of coastline the country had to offer. Whistler's Bay wasn't the Coven of the Silver Lake's commune, so as far as Nixie was concerned, it was basically purgatory.

"It isn't forever," Nixie muttered to herself. "You'll find your magic and be allowed back in the coven before you know it."

With a skin-crawling screech of its brakes, the Golden Coast Express ground to a stop. Nixie collected her things and let the other travelers push past her to the doors; she was in no hurry.

But she couldn't loiter on the train forever, and soon enough she was standing on the platform alone, blinking bitterly in the dazzling sunlight.

"Oh my stars!" an excited voice squeaked from behind her. "Look at how you've grown!"

Nixie turned and found herself face-to-face with the

spitting image of her mother. She hadn't seen her aunt Morgana in years, but with her ink black hair and wide teal eyes, there was no question that she was a Wells water witch.

Beaming, Morgana hurried forward but stopped a respectful distance away. She didn't reach out for a hug, which Nixie appreciated. Sure, the woman was taking her in, but that didn't mean she had to be happy about it.

"It's good to see you again, Nixie." Morgana smiled, a hint of sadness creeping into her features. "I'm sorry it couldn't be under better circumstances."

Rather than say something she'd regret, Nixie opted to say nothing at all. She reached for her bag, but her aunt beat her to it.

"I don't blame you for being unhappy, but I promise Whistler's Bay isn't a bad place to find your magic."

Nixie was unable to hold her tongue any longer. "That's easy for you to say. You *chose* to leave the coven."

Her aunt laughed. "I guess that's true. But don't worry, you *are* going to figure it out. I have a good feeling about you, Nixie."

"If you insist." She shrugged.

"I do," Morgana said, smiling brightly back at her. "Now come along, Malcolm is waiting with the car. He can't wait to meet you!"

Oh, right. Nixie's stomach dropped. *The human husband.*

Morgana Wells was a legend among the Coven of the Silver Lake for all the wrong reasons. Not only had she chosen to leave the commune they had called home for centuries – something Nixie could not fathom for the life of her – she had also fallen in love with a human. The last time Nixie had seen her aunt was eight years ago, the day Morgana told her family and fellow witches that she was to be married to this man. They all had been invited, but none of them had gone.

Out in the parking lot, a sturdy-looking man with broad

shoulders and a thick beard waited by an old pick-up truck. He smiled when he saw the two witches, and walked forward to greet them.

"You must be the niece I've heard so much about," he boomed, sticking out a hand. "It's a pleasure to finally meet ya, Nixie."

Having spent most of her time around other witches, Nixie often forgot about the peculiar ways humans chose to greet one another. Warily, she put her hand in Malcolm's daunting paw and gasped when he gripped, giving it a firm shake.

"Let me take those, love," he said, turning to his wife and taking the bags from her in exchange for a chaste kiss on the cheek. Nixie flushed, though she couldn't say why. "Let's get you ladies home."

'Home' was a cozy, two-bedroom cottage painted powder blue and encrusted with treasures from the sea. A wind chime of shells chattered in a salty breeze, bottles filled with sea glass caught the sunlight on the window sills, and fat white candles sat wedged into jars of sand. Nixie paused by a hand-painted driftwood sign by the front door that read *A Pretty Witch and an Old Seadog Live Here.*

Nixie pointed to the sign. "Seadog?"

Morgana laughed. "It's an expression for those who spend their lives at sea," she answered as she unlocked the front door and pushed through. "Malcolm is a fisherman. You've caught him between trips out."

"Lucky me," Nixie grumbled, taking in the cottage and all its nautical brick-a-brack. "How does a seadog end up marrying a water witch, anyway?"

Morgana smiled at her – a knowing, almost mischievous grin. "Love helps. Love of each other, love of the sea."

"And he doesn't care that you're a witch?"

"Do you think we'd have gotten married if he did?"

Nixie shrugged. "I guess not."

She wandered a bit more, out of the living room, through an open kitchen, and to a sliding glass door at the back of the house. "I've never seen the sea before."

"You're in luck," Her aunt pointed out the window to a sandy trail that disappeared through a swath of bushes at the edge of the yard. "That path will take you right to it. You should do some exploring once you've had the chance to rest – get to know the place a little. This is your home now too, after all."

She tensed involuntarily at her aunt's words. Morgana noticed.

With a gentle hand on her niece's shoulder, she turned Nixie to face her. "I know things must seem unfair right now, but everything is going to work out." Her seemingly perpetual brightness yielded to an expression of serious resolution. "I'm here to help you. Whatever you need, alright?"

Nixie looked over her shoulder. Her eyes landed on the path and she focused on it in hopes that her aunt wouldn't notice the tears she was struggling to hold back.

"What I need is–"

The front door burst open. Malcolm, arms loaded with paper grocery bags, filled the doorframe with his massive silhouette.

"Alright, ladies! Who's up for some fish fry?"

Nixie woke at sunrise the next morning.

Rather than linger and risk having to spend the morning awkwardly pretending to be interested in getting to know Morgana and Malcolm better, Nixie looked for a quiet place where she could focus on her magical studies in private. The sooner she unearthed her magical powers, the sooner she'd be able to go home.

Sliding out of the house as quiet as fog, she shuffled her way down the path behind her aunt's house. It wasn't long before she caught the sound of rolling waves. The sea couldn't be far now.

It came at her all at once; a shimmering light lept up to greet her as she crested a sandy dune. Nixie blinked, giving her eyes a moment to adjust behind the shield of her hand. When at last she was able to pull it away, the view left her breathless.

The turquoise ocean stretched out until it faded into the horizon. The color made Nixie think of her prized aquamarine gemstone – a birthday gift from her grandmother – and her heart fluttered. Small waves rolled in, reaching up the shore and licking the pristine white sands before racing out again. A rich briny scent complemented their gentle rhythm. Nixie breathed it in, feeling more awake than she had in ages.

"My stars," she whispered. "It's beautiful."

She raced down the beach, dropping her backpack and kicking off her boots. It was as though she had been transformed back into a child; she skipped into the water and wriggled her toes into the soft sand.

"Now *this* is water!" Nixie shouted, opening her arms and beaming just as widely. This seemingly endless expanse of churning seawater put the lake that gave her coven its name to shame.

"I'll say!" a voice answered.

Nixie shrieked. Turning, she spotted a girl's head bobbing above the waves not ten feet from where she stood.

"Where did you come from?" Nixie squawked. She had been certain she was alone out here only a moment ago.

The girl grinned. Her hand appeared from beneath the water and gestured to the sea. "Out there."

Before Nixie could ask what she meant, the girl slid beneath the waves. Nixie blinked and rubbed her eyes. When she opened them again, the girl was right in front of her, rising and falling with the tide. From here, Nixie could see the glimmering swish of a massive fish tail moving beneath the water.

"You're a mermaid!" Nixie exclaimed, watching as the tail made another pass, flicking close to her legs. She had heard stories about merfolk but never dreamed she would meet one in real life; she felt a little star-struck.

"And you're perceptive," the mermaid replied with a bubbling laugh. Soaked tendrils of dark cerulean hair flowed over her shoulders like meandering rivers. Her skin and eyes were different shades of deep amber, and she wore adornments of colorful shells and pearls like jewelry. She was - much to Nixie's bashful surprise - otherwise nude. Nixie averted her eyes, feeling her cheeks grow warm.

"Are you related to Morgana?"

Her question took the witch by surprise. "She's my aunt. How did you know we were related?"

"You look a lot like her with those wild eyes," she said, looking Nixie over. "You could be her as a girl. Very pretty."

"Oh." Nixie was flattered, and fiddled with the hem of her skirt to hide it. "Thank you for saying so. How do you know Morgana?"

"She comes to the water all the time," the mermaid answered as though it was the most obvious thing in the world. "That woman loves the sea almost as much as I do. I suppose you're Nixie, then?"

Again, she was taken aback. "I am. Did she... did Morgana say something about me?"

"Just that you would be staying with her for a bit. She's been very excited about it." The mermaid smiled wide, revealing

92

rows of sharp teeth. "By the way, I'm Meris."

Meris the mermaid didn't stay long. She had only come to the surface to watch the sunrise, so she bade Nixie farewell with a wink and splash.

Nixie didn't stay long either. Instead, she sprinted back to Morgana's cottage, where the inviting smells of the morning's breakfast were drifting through open windows, and burst through the door.

"I saw a mermaid!" she shouted, startling Malcolm enough that he slopped coffee down his beard.

"You've met Meris already?" Morgana sounded genuinely pleased as she scooped a generous helping of hash onto Nixie's plate. "That's wonderful. Isn't she a sweetheart?"

Malcolm pulled out the chair beside him and gave the seat a pat while Morgana, elated by her niece's excitement, put together an extra place setting.

"She said the two of you know each other?"

"I see her all the time." Morgana held the teapot with one hand and placed the other underneath it. When steam billowed from the spout, she handed the pot off to Malcolm and took her seat. "She'll often come up to sun herself in that little cove. Wonderful company. Quite the chatterbox."

Malcolm filled Nixie's cup to the brim. She gave her tea a sip – it was perfect, just the way she would have made it.

"She also said you told her about me."

"Your aunt has told anyone who would listen about you," Malcolm said with a hearty laugh. "Nothing but good things though, I promise."

Morgana beamed and Nixie blushed.

"You didn't tell her about... my problem, did you?" Nixie

was mortified just thinking about it.

"My stars, girl. No." Morgana was suddenly quite serious. "That's not my business to be sharing. If you want to tell anyone, that's your choice."

Sweet relief brought feeling back to Nixie's fingers and toes, the sense of dread lifting immediately. For the first time since she arrived, she looked at her aunt with gratitude.

"Thanks, Aunt Morgana."

Nixie didn't see Meris again for another week. By then she figured that chance meeting had been a fluke. Every day she studied in sullen silence on the beach under a wide umbrella, hoping that being close to the soothing rhythm and heady fragrance of the sea would help inspire some magic, but her lack of progress was proving to be disheartening.

"What should I try next?" she murmured as she flipped through the notes she had taken from her grandmother's grimoire. "Nana's 'Water in the Veins' visualization exercise? Ugh, never mind, I don't want to pretend I'm drowning. Maybe I could make her 'Water, Water Everywhere' talisman..."

She was reading over the supply list – a clear jar full of water, a trinket such as a river stone or seashell, myrrh to bless and consecrate the talisman, and bladderwrack for evoking water magic – when she heard a splash and looked up. There in the shallows was Meris, grinning and waving both her hands and tail fins at Nixie.

"Hello again!" she called as Nixie scrambled up to greet her.

"Hi!" Nixie was uncharacteristically giddy as she waded into the warm water. A tiny school of pearlescent fish darted between her ankles and out of her way. "I wasn't sure if I'd see you again."

"I was wondering the same thing, I've never met a witch my age before." She craned her neck to peek past Nixie. "Are you living on the beach now?"

Turning, Nixie understood how her mess of things – blankets and books, a sacked lunch and cushions, all scattered under the massive beach umbrella – looked as though she had set up camp.

"No, I've just been studying out here. I thought being closer to the water would help but–"

She froze.

Meris cocked her head. "Help with what?"

When Nixie hesitated, Meris swam past her, pulled herself onto the sand and sat up. Waves rolled in, washing around her fishy hips. Meris smiled at Nixie and patted the space beside her the way Malcolm had at breakfast on her first morning in Whistler's Bay. That long blue hair only did so much to hide the mermaid's nakedness, but Nixie was determined to be mature about it. Nixie looked down at her shorts; sitting would mean she'd get wet, but it seemed only fair given the mermaid had decided to meet her halfway.

"Tell me what's troubling you, water witch," Meris chirped.

"It's kind of embarrassing," Nixie admitted, twisting her hands anxiously.

"I promise I won't laugh."

The kind look on the mermaid's face made Nixie realize how badly she actually wanted to talk with someone about this.

"I was born into the Coven of the Silver Lake – the same one Morgana came from," she said, looking out across the water. "The witches in that coven have lived together in a commune for generations. It's like one big magical family. But because the coven is so old, we have some weird, outdated rules. One of those rules is that, if a witch hasn't developed her magical powers by the time she turns eighteen, she has to leave the coven."

"Uh oh," Meris whispered.

"Yup. You're looking at the first witch in three hundred years to be kicked out of the coven." Nixie made a grand flourish and laughed sadly.

"No offense to your coven or anything, but that's kind of intense," Meris remarked with a frown. "What now?"

"Well, I'm still a witch," Nixie said. "I come from a long, long line of Wells water witches. If I can tap into my magic, I'll be allowed go home."

Meris nodded slowly. "What do you think the problem is?"

"I have no clue." Nixie tossed her hands up in dismay and flopped backward onto the sand.

Stretching out beside her, Meris laid on her side and rested her head in her palm. "How badly do you want this?"

"More than anything," Nixie admitted quietly.

Meris hummed. "Then I wish you the best of luck, pretty Nixie."

In the weeks that followed, Meris inevitably joined Nixie every day she went to study on the beach. Sometimes the mermaid was even waiting there when she arrived.

Morgana hadn't been kidding when she said Meris was good company. The mermaid listened with true fascination as Nixie imparted her magical learnings, asking the kind of thoughtful questions that made her think long and hard to find the answers.

She also talked – a lot.

She talked about how she was the youngest in a very big family and spent most of her time bored out of her mind. She talked about how much she loved her ocean home but admitted that feeling the sun on her skin was her biggest guilty pleasure. She talked about Nixie's legs and how cute she thought her toes were. She told Nixie she had never been in love.

In return, Nixie told her about her family and how she was not-so-secretly jealous of her little sister, Rillie, for already being so much better at magic. Nixie showed Meris her prized aquamarine and told her she had never been in love either.

Meris made Nixie laugh more than she had in a very long time. Though she still hadn't made any breakthroughs with her magic, Nixie didn't feel quite as afraid about it when she was with the mermaid.

She was thinking about this – the way she felt when she spent her days at the beach with Meris – one afternoon as she waited out a summer storm.

"What's troubling you, Nix?" Morgana asked when she found her niece curled in the reading chair by the big solarium window, staring at the rain tracing down the glass.

Nixie jumped.

"Feeling homesick?" Morgana asked the question softly as she took a seat.

The question took Nixie by surprise. How long had it been since she had last pined for home?

"Not exactly," she ventured cautiously. "Aunt Morgana, can I ask you a question?"

"Of course, honey. Anything."

"What made you decide to leave the commune?"

"I fell in love with the sea." Morgana answered without even having to think about it.

"Wait, the *sea*?" Nixie sat up. "What about Malcolm?"

Her aunt smiled. "Malcolm came later. But I first left the family so I could be closer to the sea. This is my happy place. Don't get me wrong - it wasn't easy to leave the coven behind.

But, honey, magic isn't the only thing that matters. And besides, sometimes you have to make your own kind of magic instead."

Nixie ruminated on this. "Do you ever regret it?"

"I miss our family, sure," Morgana said. "But do I regret choosing my own path? Not at all."

The next day, when the sky had cleared and the sun returned to dry up all the rain, Nixie returned to the shore. Meris was already coiled on the sand, enjoying the warmth of the pristine day, and broke into a wide, sharp-toothed grin when she spotted her friend making her way over the dunes.

"I can't believe a water witch like you would hide from a little storm," she teased. "I missed you yesterday."

The candid confession made Nixie feel light as rain.

She didn't unpack her books. Instead, the witch wedged herself into the sand beside Meris, where the two spent hours talking about everything and nothing. When it got too hot, she splashed around the surf while the mermaid dove, collecting shells that she wove into Nixie's hair.

Enjoying the feeling of Meris' fingers working over her scalp, Nixie asked, "Do you remember when we first met and you told me my aunt loved the sea almost as much as you do?"

"Mm-hmm," Meris replied, still engrossed in her work.

"Morgana said it was the sea that made her leave the coven. All this time I thought it was Malcolm. What do you think makes the sea so special?"

Meris silently weaved a scallop shell above Nixie's ear as she considered the question.

"That's a tough one," she admitted. "What I love about it is likely very different than what a water witch loves about it."

"Well then, what are some of your favorite things about

it?"

"I could tell you." Meris smiled that mischievous grin of hers. "But maybe it would be more fun if I *showed* you instead."

"Really?" Nixie gaped, hardly able to believe her luck. "How?"

To Nixie's surprise, Meris blushed, her cheeks grew dark instead of red. "Well, it might actually be a little awkward."

"Awkward how?"

"I can share my breath with you, just for a little while. You'd be able to see the water the way I do. But..." Meris bit her lip and glanced away. "I'd need to kiss you."

Nixie faltered, just for a moment. This would be her first kiss. She looked at Meris, imagined what her lips might feel like against her own, and smiled.

"Okay, let's do it."

Surprise quickly gave way to giddy excitement as Meris pushed back into deeper water and gestured for Nixie to follow. The witch waded in until she could no longer feel the sandy ocean floor beneath her feet.

"Are you ready?" Meris asked.

When Nixie nodded, Meris took her by the hips, pulled her close, and kissed her gently. The mermaid's lips were slick and salty as they slid across Nixie's slowly, sending a shudder racing through her body. Nixie's heart hammered. It might have been the result of whatever magic Meris was working, but she suspected it was something else entirely.

The kiss made her feel weak. It made her want more. As if by instinct, Nixie moved into it, draping her arms around Meris' neck, desperate for their closeness to last.

It wasn't until Nixie pulled back, flustered in the best way, that she realized she and Meris were now completely submerged beneath the waves. Without thinking, she gasped at the world around her, but the water only swirled in her mouth without reaching her throat.

"Come on!" Meris laughed, taking Nixie by the hand. She pulled her along as she pumped her powerful tail, cutting through the water with ease. Nixie gazed around, awestruck by the beauty of the mermaid's world.

Gauzy streams of sunlight cut through the water's surface, casting dancing spotlights along the rippled sand below. Schools of electric-hued fish darted amid the flowering reefs. Meris brought them closer so Nixie could see the fluttering of their delicate fins as the fish moved as a single entity. Meris pointed down at a massive sea turtle drifting with the motion of the water. The ancient creature craned its neck, peering up at the pair with inky black eyes.

Meris drew them out further to where the sea grew murky and cold. Suspended in the middle of such vastness, Nixie thought this must have been what it was like to fly.

Out from the gloom materialized a colossal shape; a whale – the biggest living creature the witch had ever seen – swam by as though in slow motion. Nixie's eyes were wide in silent wonder, mesmerized by the animal's grace and soulful song.

But as beautiful as the underwater world was, it all paled compared to Meris. Nixie floated, transfixed by the soft cloud of the mermaid's hair and the way her tail fins wafted and swirled in the current. Even in the dim light of the depths, she shone. Under the water, Nixie's heartbeat felt like a series of crashing waves.

Meris caught her staring, and her amber cheeks went dark.

It was all over too soon for Nixie. Before the magic breath ran out, Meris dragged her back to the surface and led her to shore.

"That was amazing!" Nixie cried as she stumbled, laughing, onto the beach, vibrating with excitement. "Absolutely incredible!"

"Do you get it now?" Meris grinned up at her. "Do you see why your aunt and I love it so much?''

"Yes!" Nixie said, exhilarated by what she had seen. The feeling bubbled up from somewhere deep inside her until she felt ready to burst. "Meris! I think... I think I'm ready!"

Standing with her feet in the water and hands out before her, Nixie called on everything: from the first moment she saw the sea to the world she had witnessed beneath the waves. She thought about Meris; how grateful she was for the mermaid's company and how much she appreciated that she had shared her magnificent home. She thought about how beautiful she looked, wrapped in the depths of the sea, and how special that first kiss had been to her - even if had just been a means to an end.

The memory of Meris' lips on hers was so fresh, she swore she could still feel them there, giving her breath instead of taking it away. She licked her lips and tasted salt.

Nixie's heart hammered.

Raising her palms to face one another, Nixie poured all of this into the space between her hands. She imagined water swirling and condensing. If this worked, Nixie would see a tiny, storming rain cloud rolling before her when she opened her eyes.

She took another breath. In her mind, it was water – not blood – coursing through her veins.

From somewhere that sounded hundreds of miles away, Nixie heard a rumble and a gasp.

Her eyes snapped open and there it was: a dark, flashing storm cloud suspended between her palms. It was a perfect tempest in miniature and when Nixie flicked her wrists, it let loose a downpour of tiny raindrops that fell into the ocean until it rained itself into oblivion.

"You did it!" Meris laughed. "You found your magic!"

Nixie shrieked. She looked from Meris to her hands and

back. She shrieked again and threw her arms around the mermaid, the pair laughing until they were out of breath.

When at last they pulled apart, Meris' eyes swam with tears.

"Congratulations," she said, squeezing Nixie's hands in her own. "I guess this means you get to go home."

For the first time that summer, the idea of going back to her familiar cabin by the lake didn't make Nixie happy. She looked at Meris, radiant even in the fading light of day, and imagined not seeing her again after tonight.

That didn't make her happy, either.

"Well, I don't have to leave right away."

Meris gaped. "What are you talking about?" She balked, shaking her head in disbelief. "I thought this was what you wanted?"

"I thought so too," Nixie agreed, feeling bold. "But now I'm not so sure."

"What do you mean?" Meris asked carefully, her body freezing in place as if one wrong move might prove this all to be a dream.

"I think I would miss the sea too much if I left now," Nixie said, leaning in. "And I know I'd miss you. So what's the hurry?"

The mermaid's eyes sparkled with delight.

"I'd like it if you stayed," Meris whispered. "My pretty water witch."

Nixie closed the distance between them, and with this kiss she knew she had found a happy place of her own.

MAGGIE DERRICK is a bisexual writer, artist, and professional dog-petter from Vancouver, Canada. Her first novel, *The Star and the Ocean*, was a winner in the 2017 Watty Awards. Find her at maggiederrick.com, and on Twitter as @MaggieDerrick.

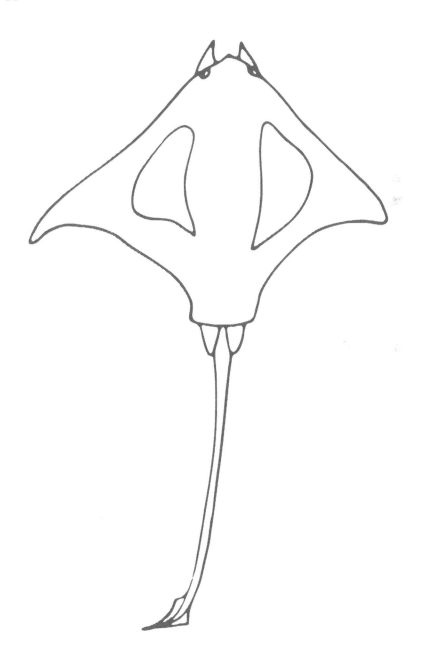

FAMILIAR WATERS

by V. S. Holmes

Silt dusted the walls of the cave, memories in the corners of a mind. Glittering. Weightless. The sound of water passing the cave's mouth was no longer the languid murmur of summer over sun-hot cobbles. Iguaçu uncurled from the warmth of the mud, swirling and stretching, shaking sand from her skin. Beside her, Bia did not stir, but her gills fluttered faintly, smooth scales expanding in rest. The brown whiskers framing Bia's mouth felt the change in the water as her lover rose, and she settled back into the warmth of the mud. Iguaçu smiled. Bia was not an early riser.

The river spirit wove through the tangle of kapok roots enclosing their home. It was dawn. Mist rose from Iguaçu's surface, breath eddying through the tree trunks along her shore. As much as habit drove her to patrol her banks, she dallied. This morning was different from the others. *The rains end today.*

Despite how her waters danced, Iguaçu's heart was heavy. Summer was over. That night, with all her kinfolk, Bia would leave.

Iguaçu was no longer the jealous, swift river she once was.

She knew Bia would swim in different rivers, ones tasting of the ocean's tang, and others that were steady and so broad she could not see one bank from the other. But she would return. Iguaçu was the water of Bia's home.

"Good morning, Çu."

Iguaçu turned, smiling at the nickname. "I didn't mean to wake you."

Bia's scales rippled in a gentle shrug. "It's hard to sleep the night before a Voyage." Her eyes were the deep brown of river mud, dotted with gold, like silt. "So many thoughts from my people, and they crowd my mind. They're excited."

Iguaçu watched her lover creep from the coziness of the mud. Shafts of sunlight warmed the spirit's waters, and ignited the iridescence in Bia's dapples, turned her pale belly pearlescent. "I thought I heard the toucan fledglings learning to fly yesterday."

Iguaçu nodded, unwilling to interrupt the soft sound of Bia's voice.

"This is their fourth clutch here, I think. Maybe fifth. Soon the chicks will have their own nests above your banks." She stretched, fins fluttering faster now in the sun's warmth. "Though I would appreciate if they understood the concept of sleeping in."

Iguaçu chuckled, the sound already carrying autumn's sharpness.

Bia swirled in the eddy of her lover's laugh. "Do you remember when we first met?"

Iguaçu did. "My banks were narrow and steep. The hills were mountains, and the prairie not yet grown over by trees." She smiled. The world had been different; great saber-cats and giant sloths grazing where tapir and monkeys now roamed. "You were younger too, leading your kin to my waters." She caressed Bia's dappled scales, smooth from the wear of time.

"And I tried to make you come with me in winter."

106

"And I tried to make you stay." Iguaçu dove into the cold of the deep channel now, feeling Bia follow, fins fluttering, body sinuous along the sand. "I did not realize what made you leave is what made me love you, then."

Bia's expression grew wistful. "Swim with me?" It was their tradition on the last day of summer.

Iguaçu curled around Bia's fin. "Until the hills are plains and my banks are dry."

The day still held enough of summer to make Iguaçu warm, her current slow and peaceful. They wove through the cool pockets of weeds, rested in the mud along her curves. Iguaçu led them past the soft noses of capybara and under the shadow of the ever-present jaguar. Already the echo of the falls rumbled ahead. Bia slowed. It was not time to visit the falls, not yet. Not until tonight. Iguaçu felt Bia's family stirring, gathering. She looked back at the catfish goddess. Bia's gaze was distant.

"What are you thinking of?" Iguaçu asked.

"We are fewer than we used to be. And the waters are changing. Not just yours."

"They change every year," Iguaçu pointed out. The animal gods came long after the spirits of the rocks and rivers. Bia was old, but not as old as Iguaçu.

The river lived through many changes in her pocket of the rainforest. One of those changes brought Bia and her people swimming up her waters. *What if, one day, another change keeps them away?*

Bia turned, her eyes catching the sorrow in Iguaçu's. "Çu." Her tone softened. She moved closer, whiskers caressing Iguaçu's eddies, memorizing the details of her banks and curves. Tenderness drove away Iguaçu's concern. They did not speak, but Iguaçu felt the flutter of promise through Bia's skin. *I'll come back.* Iguaçu wrapped herself around Bia, feeling the strength of her fins before pulling away. Shadows stretched from her western banks now. Their time was short. "Come home with me? Just until dusk?"

Bia smiled, flushed with love and impending adventure. "Always."

The cave was quiet. Silt and sand still eddied from their love-making. Iguaçu watched Bia rise. The goddess's muscles tensed with anticipation. It was as if Iguaçu's touch had stripped the stillness from her lover's skin. Now Bia hummed with energy. In the moon-dappled water beyond, her kinfolk waited. She pressed a fin to Iguaçu cheek, but did not say a word, as if her approaching journey swallowed her voice first.

Iguaçu did not mind. They did not need words. She followed the catfish goddess into the deeper channel. Their kapok's branches were lace across the moon's face. Already, Iguaçu current quickened, rising water kissing Bia's skin as it carried her towards the falls. The cataracts had multiplied, swollen with summer's rain. The rumble turned to thunder, then a deafening roar. Iguaçu paused at the crest of the tallest, clinging to the rocks as her waters rushed past and over into the mist below. She turned to Bia, poised beside her, body taut. They kissed again, not a goodbye, but almost.

Clear membranes slid over Bia's gold irises, and she turned and pitched herself into the current. The moonlight slid along the sinuous backs of Bia's kin. They crowded about her, surging after their goddess. Iguaçu wrapped herself around roots, holding back from flooding after them into the next river's roaring waters. A river cannot weep, but Iguaçu swore her current was saltier. *Until spring, beautiful voyager.*

The moon set, leaving her waters so dark she could taste it.

It was not dawn, but she could not rest. Her cave was too empty, the mud too cold, the walls too dull without the light shining off Bia's scales. Roots cramped her banks and she ripped herself away, white froth spattering her surface. Water jabbered, the vanguard to winter's chatter.

Beyond, Bia swam, gliding out into the icy dark, with only deep blue-black ahead.

Iguaçu changed from its burble and snap to a desperate trickle, more mud than water. Animals that often made her waters their home moved east in favor of deeper water, wider banks. Such things happened during winter. But something was different this year. Iguaçu had not heard the jaguar's call in a long time. She never counted days – the kapok tree did not count centuries, or rocks millennia. Now she wondered if she should start. Winter seemed to last forever. Her waters grew warm, the mud at the edges dull, cracked like the reflection of the moon on her surface. Still, the rains did not come. The toucans made their first nest – only a single egg. Hoya hanging from the trees shriveled, waxy petals curled shut before they could bloom. Clouds did not gather.

Then the kapok fell. The groan and scream of wounded wood drowned out the cries of startled howlers as they scattered. She churned, as much from confusion as disruption and grief. She surged to the surface, staring at the broken roots, the thirsty, yellowed leaves. The tapir god paused at the battered, shattered trunk, where the green wood was sick and bright.

"What happened?" She realized now it was not her impatience making the rain seem late. *The weather's changed.*

"There's not enough water. What nutrients are left are locked in the mud." His dark eyes held resignation. "Our sisters tell me there's water closer to the ocean, but the storms there beat the trees and waves too fiercely. Our brothers in the mountains say winter comes sooner, and lasts longer each year."

Her heart ached, but she tried to hide the fear from her eyes.

The tapir god's expression softened. "The rain will come, I'm sure. It's just late."

Later every year, though. Waves trembled against her banks. *If there's not enough water for the kapok, for the animals, how can Bia come home?* She did not speak it aloud, too afraid it would echo in the ripple of her water and become truth. When she was able to see through the shaking surface, the tapir god was gone, too, his tracks leading east.

That night as she drifted, quiet under the no-moon sky, she dreamt of darkness and the cool brush of a brown fin.

Sand settled between Iguaçu's toes. Mud clogged the entrance to her cave, filling the gaps left by the uprooted kapok tree. The days wore on and the sun rose early, warming her waters and painting her banks with light. Her patrol took her past the new toucan nest, between the roots of the saplings encroaching on her backwaters, under the rotting length of her tree. A new island rose from her winter-low waters downstream, already home to sunning capybara and caimans. She pushed out farther, waters curling with the force.

The falls were a faint mutter, steady and slow. A second rumble joined, this one from the sky. Then again, closer. Fish and salamander rushed past, tucking themselves into crevices and under rocks. *Crack-boom.* Iguaçu rushed upriver, peering at the mountains suddenly shrouded in thick, clotted clouds.

Rain! The water inched up her banks, then surged forward, white and full of mountain flavor. Iguaçu forgot how it felt to have her heart race, her banks reshaped under the hopeful hands of summer. Her current rushed towards the ocean. At the falls she stopped and curled against a sun-warmed rock. She strained to see through the mist and clouded water.

There! Dapples flashed, the flick of brown scales through churning water. Iguaçu grinned. She tasted the ocean's salt, the cold of deeper waters carried upriver. Now sunlight struck sparkles from the backs of Bia's kin. Not the thousands that left, but a hundred. Between scores of flashing fins, Iguaçu picked out the dappled curve of her lover's body. She rushed forward, reaching down the tumbling falls to brush closer to Bia as she leapt up and up and up. The goddess finally surged over the rocks, gills heaving, sides full and strong from swimming in foreign waters.

Iguaçu paused, eddying and shy for a moment. Her heart thundered like the falls in summer, threatening to overflow her banks from joy and relief. She had myriad questions for her lover about the different skies she had swum beneath, the different fish she had seen. When Bia's gaze finally settled on her, however, the questions stilled.

The goddess's mouth curled into a bright smile, brighter than the gold flecking her eyes. She reached out a fin. "Swim with me?"

V. S. HOLMES is a gender-queer contract archaeologist and the author of *Reforged* and the *Nel Bently Books*. *Smoke and Rain*, the first in her fantasy quartet, was chosen for New Apple Literary's 2015 Excellence in Independent Publishing Award. She can be found online at vsholmes.com, facebook.com/authorvsholmes, and @VS_Holmes.

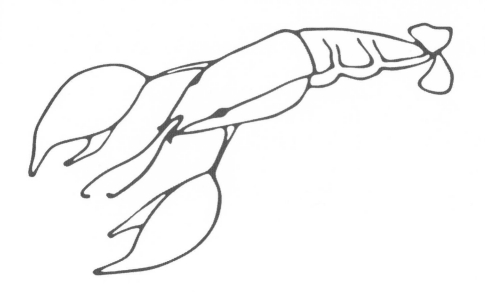

TANNER AND THE WATER NYMPH

by Jaylee James

"I shouldn't care so much," Tanner told emself, furrowing er brows into a scowl to form the shape e wanted – straight, masculine, with no arch – before sweeping the thin angled brush through them. *Small strokes, a light hand, mimic the shape of natural hairs.* "It's just *Lily*."

E didn't even like Lily. She was one of those white girls whose style was a hodge podge of appropriated cultures, with the scent of Etsy-bought incense and weed smoke clinging to her organic cotton maxi skirts, and long hair tangling over tattoos in languages she couldn't even pronounce properly.

But Lily was into "all that witchy spiritual stuff," as their mutual friend Max had pointed out over coffee, "and could probably fix your haunted shower."

"It's not haunted." Tanner kept insisting, but each time e said it, it sounded less true.

"Maintenance has looked at it three times, yeah? And there's nothing wrong with it." Max had leaned over the table, too energetic at eight A.M. "Nothing in *this realm* at least."

Er hand lingered over the electric razor, debating whether or not the fuzzy scruff on either side of er head was long enough

113

to warrant a buzz. *It's just Lily. There's no reason to get all boyed up for her.*

It's not like she'd even notice.

Tanner shoved the razor away, let it clatter around in the sink, loud over er own thoughts.

A peppy, musical knock resounded on the cheap apartment door.

"Coming," e called, sweeping all the makeup into a drawer.

Lily's face split into a smile when Tanner opened the door. "Hey girl!"

Wince.

"Hey, Lily." E endured a bracing, one-armed hug before letting her into er apartment. It was just one room, a former hotel refurbished for starving college kids and the underemployed. "The bathroom's right there."

"Straight to it, then!" Lily kicked off her beaded sandals and stepped barefoot onto Tanner's tile floor.

"Do you need anything? Or, like... I have soda."

"I don't do processed sugar, hon, but thanks."

"Right. Sorry."

Lily hopped up to sit on Tanner's counter, closing her eyes and reaching both hands out toward the shower, humming lightly.

"I can definitely feel a strong energy in this space." Lily's voice was lilting and dreamy, eyes still closed. "But this is your *boudoir*, where you perform the everyday rituals to protect you in the outside world."

"My what?"

Lily moved to the shower, touching the water-stained chrome fixtures with reverence. "If a soul truly is lingering here, it means they likely died in this tub." She traced a finger along the edge and Tanner wished e had spent the afternoon scrubbing it down instead of fussing with er appearance.

"You know who dies alone in a hotel bathtub?" Lily's voice dropped low and sad as she turned to Tanner with mournful eyes. "Suicides."

"Uh..." E rasped er hand over the shaved shape of er skull. "That's kinda dark, don't you think?"

"Please, Sarah, I need–"

"It's Tanner."

"Ohmygod, sorry, sorry. You're right. Ugh, I suck so much. It's just so hard to remember, you know? Tanner. *Tanner, Tanner, Tanner, Tanner*–"

"*Stop*." The name – *er* name, which usually made er heart soar each time e heard it – sounded so wrong in Lily's mouth. "Look, I've got some things to work on, so how about I leave you to it?"

"Sorry..." Lily's face crumpled and she twisted her hands in her skirt. "Are you mad at me?"

"No, I'm not mad at you." Tanner needed a nap after this. Maybe a hundred naps.

"I really am trying with the whole, you know... *Tanner thing.* It's just, I've known you for so long, and–"

Tanner was not playing this game today. "I do actually have stuff to do, though, so I'll be in the other room. You'll probably work better without me breathing down your neck anyway."

E left, not pausing for Lily's protests. E settled at a TV tray with er laptop. There was no "stuff to do," but e lifted the lid and stared at er web browser anyway.

Lily lit incense, played music, chanted nonsense, and called out to the spirit again and again. "Oh, restless spirit, listen to my voice. Hear my longing to meet you, to speak with you and

115

ease your burden. I beseech you, lost soul, as a mutual sufferer of existence, to commune with me in this– AAHH!!"

Lily screamed, a piercing shriek above the sudden thump and clatter.

"Lily!" E ran to the bathroom. "Are you okay?"

She was petrified, hands over her mouth, crouched half-in and half-out of Tanner's sink.

E followed her gaze to the shower...

And to the being crouched in the middle of er tub.

"I'm here," it said. "So you can stop chanting at me."

At first, all Tanner could really see was the creature's hair. It was so long, it covered everything like a drape, pooled in the tub like black water, and spilled over the sides in dark, fluid strands. And it was wet, clinging to green-brown skin the color of algae and mud.

"What *are* you?" Lily's voice shook, shrill and wild. "You look like the girl from *The Ring*. Get back, demon!"

Lily threw a still-smoking sage stick into the shower.

It hissed as it hit damp skin. When the creature flinched back, Tanner realized under all that hair was a girl. A naked, too-thin girl, shivering from the damp or from fear.

Immediately, e felt like a complete ass for thinking of her as a *creature*.

"Hey, um..." Tanner pulled er bath towel from its rung and held it out to the girl. "Here."

She held herself tighter, hands digging into her skin where she clutched her own elbows.

"I'm not going to hurt you. It's just a towel. You look kinda cold."

The girl widened her already enormous eyes – solemn, dark, with a ripple of green beneath the surface – and said, "Oh." A single note holding too much open joy for such a small gesture.

116

Lily was still curled up on the counter, finally quiet as she watched the girl drape the thin towel over her body and hair like a cape.

"Thank you, kind sir."

Tanner's face went hot. "You're... welcome, I guess."

The bathroom held completely still for the space of one breath.

And then chaos erupted in multiple directions.

"I'll leave." The girl moved forward.

"Stay away from me!" Lily shrieked, half-jumping, half-falling off the counter, stuff clattering everywhere as she threw herself towards the door.

"Lily, calm down!"

But she shoved Tanner against the wall, knocking the wind out of em as she ran past.

The girl tripped over the lip of the tub, all her solemn grace vanishing as she grabbed for the shower curtain to catch her fall. Decorative beaded hoops scraped across the shower rod before it popped out of the wall completely.

The door to Tanner's apartment slammed shut with a thud.

The curtain rod hit Tanner in the face.

And the girl and all of her hair collapsed onto Tanner's bathroom tile, partly wrapped in a polyethylene copy of the periodic table.

"Well," Tanner wheezed, catching er breath. "That just happened."

"The first name the humans gave me was Okchamali'."
When she said the name, Tanner saw her smile for the first time. "It was their people's word for *green*."

117

But Tanner, she conceded, could call her Mali.

It turned out Mali wasn't a ghost. She was a water nymph – a minor deity tied to a body of water, who acted as its caregiver, who died if she did not have any water to take care of.

And who, quite frankly, was being extremely melodramatic about the whole thing.

"Just go. Leave me." She curled up inside her own hair, her voice a high-pitched whine. "Leave me here to wither and die."

Tanner squatted on the bathroom floor, peering into Mali's face like she was one of er students throwing a tantrum. "Mali," e said in er calm, soothing counselor voice. "I'm not going to leave you. For one thing, this is my bathroom. And also, I'm not really a fan of things dying, like, in general. So can we figure this out?"

The voice was working. Mali peered up at er through parted fingers.

"If I'm understanding you correctly, your main problem today is that you need a body of water to live in. I'm assuming that was my shower up until Lily annoyed you into leaving it. Am I following?"

Mali's hands fell away from her face and she stared at em, open-mouthed, as if e were revealing all the secrets of the universe to her.

Years of training was all that kept em from chuckling under er breath. Who knew active listening skills worked the same on supernatural creatures as they did on high schoolers?

"Yes," she finally answered em. "But my pond–"

"Does it have to be the pond?"

"I *need* my pond."

"But you were in the shower just fine. For at least two weeks."

Mali stared blankly at em until e gestured at the shower itself.

"Oh. That. Yes. I live in water, any size or shape... It's not home, not bonded to me in a way that gives me life, but..."

"But it will do? At least until tomorrow?"

"Yes. I can return to the... *shower*."

"No!" Tanner scrubbed a hand over er hair. "I have a better idea. How about a fish tank?"

"A what?"

Tanner lead her back into the main room of er apartment, where a twenty gallon fish tank took up most of the space beneath the wall-mounted television.

"Oh!" Mali squealed, clapping her hands in delight. "Snails!"

"Yeah, too many snails. The internet has at least a dozen ways to kill them, but I just..."

Mali's big, round eyes stared at em, waiting. Tanner sighed.

"They're trapped in there. I can't just kill them. It would be cruel."

"*Tanner*." Mali beamed at em, saying er name with too much meaning.

The glass walls of the tank were clouded with algae, the gravel half made up of empty snail shells, with a thick forest of aquatic plants filling most of the space. Between the greenery flashed thin, narrow fish, while one female betta, a crimson curl of elegant fins, relaxed on a leaf near the surface of the water.

"I know it needs cleaning... The algae is gross, and–"

"Algae is a plant." Mali stated everything like a royal pronouncement.

"Well, yeah, but–"

When Tanner looked up again, Mali was gone.

"Hello?" E spun around, glancing around the apartment for signs of her. The bathroom was empty, and e hadn't heard the door open.

She was just... gone.

119

The next afternoon, after Tanner had already worked three hours at Parkville Middle School, and another three at its high school counterpart, it was hard for em to believe Mali had been anything but er imagination.

E'd texted Lily to see if she was okay, and got a nasty text back, blaming Tanner for pulling some kind of elaborate prank on her.

"Hey, weird question..." Tanner asked the receptionist as e logged out for lunch. "Do you know about any ponds in the area being... destroyed, I guess? Drained?"

"Sorry, Sarah, I haven't."

E bit er tongue. "Thanks anyway."

"Um... Mixer Evans?"

Tanner beamed at the teenage boy who'd said er name. "Hey, Asher. It's just pronounced 'Mix,' but it means a lot that you remembered to use it."

Asher blushed and shoved his bangs down into his face with a scowl. "Whatever. You asked about a pond, yeah? They're trashing the one in my neighborhood to build some kind of strip mall."

"Thanks, man. That's good to know!"

The boy grumbled under his breath and shuffled out of the office, but Tanner couldn't help but smile. The kid's social anxiety was something they'd been working on all semester. Just a few months ago, Asher never would have spoken up like that, especially not with two authority figures.

Progress.

It gave Tanner enough hope to smile on the way to er shift at the other high school across town.

After work, Tanner was apprehensive about what e might find in er apartment. But it was empty.

No moon-eyed girls with fluid grace and a greenish tinge to their brown skin.

No Mali.

Frankly, e wasn't sure if e should be worried or relieved.

"The water's too acidic."

"Aahh!" Tanner stumbled back, falling awkwardly onto er bed.

Mali peered down at em, head cocked in curiosity.

"What the hell, Mali?!"

She rolled one elegant shoulder in a shrug. "Pebbles doesn't mind the water, but the schools... Hufflefluff? And the other one... Some kind of bird..."

"How did you know what I named my fish?"

"They told me."

"Okay, better question. How do my *fish* know what their names are?"

A strand of Mali's hair slid free from behind her ear and fell softly against Tanner's cheek.

"They listen when you talk to them, Tanner." If she'd been one of er students, she would have rolled her eyes.

E scrambled off the bed to peer into the tank, which was now...

"You cleaned the tank?"

"Oh, that was the snails. This generation will be well-fed on algae and plant detritus, but the next will be more controlled, I think..." She threw a smile Tanner's way. "You said there were too many of them. I agree. There aren't enough plants to keep up with their waste. But if they gorge themselves on algae this cycle, their children will face a scarcity of resources, and..." Something in Tanner's expression made Mali duck her head behind a veil of hair. "The water's too acidic."

And before er eyes, the girl seemed to shimmer, then dissolve into the air itself.

"Pebbles is the queen. Indisputably so. I'm not sure if she's shy, or just lazy, but all she ever does is lay on her leaf and watch the snails." Mali huffed, but it was too affectionate to have any real heat behind it. "Sometimes she will follow one snail across the glass, or gently nudge them with her face."

Tanner watched the nymph as she sat cross-legged on er bed, hands expressive as she spoke about er fish – *Tanner's fish* – with all the excitement of a child on her first day of school.

"If Pebbles is the queen, are the snails her subjects?"

"Oh, undoubtedly. The schools are skittish by nature, and avoid her whenever they can, but the snails don't mind. They trust her."

Plastic crinkled as Tanner gently removed the driftwood logs e had bought at the pet store. A freckle-faced cashier had assured em the logs would balance the water's acidity, and they made Mali's eyes light up the minute she saw them, so Tanner figured it was a good decision.

"However." Mali's voice grew soft. "It's lonely to be the only one of your kind in the water. The snails have each other, and so do the schools. But Pebbles has no one."

"Mali–"

The nymph twinkled out of sight before Tanner could respond.

"That fish is much too large for a pond." Mali scrunched her nose at the television. "I'm glad. Pebbles wouldn't stand a chance."

After Mali had grasped the concept of video footage and television, she had become immediately fascinated by Shark Week.

"And you enjoy these shows? Seeing predators like this doesn't bother you?"

Tanner shrugged. "It's not like we live anywhere near the ocean."

Her small feet barely reached the foot of the bed, and her cascade of dark hair laid cool and silky against Tanner's arm. E tried to focus on er work, but found er gaze drifting to Mali's fascinated expression too often to make any real progress.

Tanner chewed er ham and cheese sandwich in er cramped office and scrolled through photos on a local aquarium shop's Facebook page. E'd found a store boasting a tank of cohabitating female bettas – which was apparently rarer than Tanner had expected when starting the search – and now had dozens of photos of beautiful, if overpriced, designer fish to sort through.

I should get Mali's advice, e thought to emself. *She'd know what kind of fish would make an excellent co-queen.*

The thought conjured an image of Pebbles in a fur-lined cape, booping snails with a tiny scepter to knight them. Tanner couldn't help but sputter a laugh.

"You seem happier these days."

E hadn't realized e had an audience.

"Was I unhappy before?"

"I wouldn't say unhappy. Just... tired."

Max stood in the doorway. He and Tanner had both worked at the high school for two years now, and he was probably the closest thing Tanner had to a best friend.

"We work with teenagers all day. Pretty sure we're all *tired*."

He offered Tanner a courtesy laugh at er joke, but shook his head. "Not like you do. You're always here early and leaving late. You give those kids your all, every single day."

Tanner shoved more of the sandwich into er mouth to keep from having to respond.

"You take such good care of these kids." He smiled at em. "I'm glad you've found someone to take care of *you* for once."

E nearly choked on er sandwich.

"Found someone? I haven't... It's not like you're thinking."

"Uh-huh." Max gave em a wink. "Whatever it is, it's definitely making you smile a lot more."

Together, they'd chosen an ice-white betta so pale that she glowed blue under the tank's nighttime setting.

"Do you think she'll like her new friend?" Tanner's face was so close to Mali's, both of them staring into the tank as the two bettas swam around each other. "The guy at the shop gave me this divider we can use if they start fighting."

"They won't." Mali smiled at em. "I'll make sure of it."

This time, when the nymph glittered into the tank, Tanner couldn't help but smile.

"I haven't been in human form for a long, long time."

Tanner cursed under er breath. E felt like e should be used to this by now, the way Mali appeared out of thin air with no warning, in the middle of a thought, as if she'd been talking to em this whole time.

"What?"

"Hundreds of years, I think. Nymphs, dryads, nature spirits... we used to live with humans in their villages, take meals with them, be their friends." She tilted her head, staring at Tanner's laptop the way some people stare dreamily at the horizon. "But I'm not sure I remember how."

When Tanner said nothing, just frowned deeper in confusion, Mali sighed.

"You wanted to know if I eat or need to sleep. Yesterday, remember?"

Tanner remembered voicing those thoughts to emself, in er empty apartment. But er apartment was never truly empty anymore.

"Ah." Tanner cleared er throat. "Would you... *like* to eat? And sleep?"

Mali considered a moment, then nodded decisively.

"I'll make dinner tomorrow, then. Real dinner, not–" E gestured vaguely at the greasy remains of er frozen pizza. "I only have the one bed, though."

"Oh. I had thought... The villagers, they often shared one bed. Sometimes an entire family."

"Yeah, that makes sense. Um..." Tanner stretched out er legs, the thin boxers and t-shirt e wore suddenly feeling a lot thinner at the idea of Mali joining em in bed.

125

She braided her hair with nervous fingers, avoiding Tanner's eyes. "It's okay if you don't want to. I can—"

"I want to."

E stared at the ceiling for most of the night, listening to Mali's heartbeat, feeling the coolness of her presence in er bed. She was so soft, and so *small*, and her long braid curled around Tanner's limbs as if it was trying to hold em down.

How long had it been since Tanner was close enough to touch another person?

Mali wasn't the only one who'd forgotten how to be with someone.

Tanner's apartment didn't have a kitchen, but e had an electric skillet and a panini press hissing with heat, filling up the room with the scents of spice and melting cheese. Mali perched on the bed, watching the process with the same intensity she held for Shark Week.

It wasn't until they sat eating over fold-out TV trays that Mali said, "I need a pond."

Tanner went very, very still.

"Oh?"

"I need to bond to water of my own again." She tore apart her garlic bread without eating it. "I appreciate your fish tank, but I need a home."

Cold wrapped around Tanner's heart and gave a hard squeeze.

"Yeah. You said that. When we first met, you told me you

needed something more."

"I can already feel myself growing weaker. Without bonding, having water to care for, I will eventually die."

Tanner imagined Mali in her element, tending to the cattails, encouraging the baby ducks, guiding the tadpoles through their life cycles. E pictured the delighted face she made when telling em about Pebbles and the snails. How much brighter would her smile be with a full water bond?

How could e ever stop her from having that?

"When were you planning on leaving?"

Mali frowned. "I'm not sure. I haven't found a place to go."

"Good." Tanner coughed. "I mean, if you need help, I could try looking for you. I'm sure there are parks that have–"

With a frustrated huff, Mali winked from sight, leaving her dinner mostly untouched.

Tanner gently set the travel mug of tank water in er cupholder as Mali settled into the passenger seat of er car.

She crossed her arms tightly over her chest, refusing to look at em as they pulled out of the parking lot, but soon she was leaning forward, pointing at everything and shouting with delight as the city flew past their windows.

"There are so many houses!" she cried, pointing to a grocery store.

"Not every building is a house, Mali... Some of those are shops, or offices, or–"

"Look at all those birds! Do you think the air has nymphs as well?"

"How should I know? That's your area of expertise."

With every giddy exclamation, Tanner's heart thudded

hotter in er chest, torn between overwhelming affection and terror at what e was losing.

The surface of Lake Cordelia sparkled as a breeze Tanner couldn't feel threw rough texture across its surface. According to the internet, it was manmade, a patch of tightly-controlled nature wrapped in a wealthy suburb.

E'd spent hours poring over online maps and park service websites. Each lake, pond, and stream was rejected immediately. Nothing e found was good enough for Mali.

But Lake Cordelia was beautiful, its web page providing detailed information about the kinds of fish that lived in its waters and plenty of photos of young children splashing along the shore. Mali deserved a lake that children would dip their toes into.

E swallowed the lump in er throat and told emself e wouldn't cry.

"Tanner?" Mali's voice was barely audible over the wind. "I don't have to go."

"Yes you do. You need water to care for. I can't let you fade away in my apartment until there's nothing left of you."

Waves crashed around the lake as though it were an ocean.

"You said you needed to bond."

"I do."

E forced a clumsy gesture at the lake in front of them. "So bond."

Mali's frown deepened into a vicious scowl. "With the lake? I don't want this lake, Tanner."

"What, is it not good enough for you?" E clenched er teeth. "Sorry, I don't mean to snap at you. This was the best lake I could find in the area. I tried so hard to find something you would like, something close enough that I could visit you, but−"

"Tanner. Have you thought about kissing me?"

Tanner nearly choked on nothing but air. "What would possess you to ask a question like that?"

She visibly deflated, shoulders drooping. "So you haven't."

E took a step toward her, then stopped himself. "I have."

"Have you thought about kissing me while you're supposed to be working?"

"Yes."

"And staring at the ceiling when you can't fall asleep?" When e didn't answer, Mali took another step toward em. "Have you thought about kissing me then?"

"Yes."

"With your heart racing and your blood rushing in your ears and heat crashing through you anytime you picture yourself doing it?"

Tanner's cheeks were flaming. E ducked er head, ruffling er hair with er hand. "I don't know about all that..."

"Oh." Mali seemed to shrink even smaller.

They were standing close enough, Tanner could reach out and touch her if e tried.

Reach out and kiss her, even.

"So you don't want to kiss me. Not that much."

She took a step back and e said, "Wait. Please," before e even knew it was coming out of er mouth.

Mali took it back, moved closer instead, waiting just as e had asked.

"Yes." Er voice was a whisper. "To all of that. Yes."

Her small, brown hands fiddled with the hem of er jacket, and she looked up at em with enormous, green-brown eyes. "So will you?"

Without breaking eye contact, Mali took Tanner's cold

hands in hers. She lifted them to her face, using Tanner's hands to cup her own cheeks.

E couldn't breathe.

"Will you kiss me?"

"Oh, *shit*," Tanner whispered before e swayed forward, pulled Mali's face the rest of the way to er own, and kissed her.

Slow, and thorough, and deep.

With er heart racing, and the blood rushing in er ears, and heat crashing through em as e lost emself in the feel of her mouth, cold from where the wind had kissed her before Tanner had gotten the chance.

Er voice was a ragged sound as e dropped both er arms around Mali's body and held her tight, as close as e could with layers of thick winter clothing between them.

Tanner kissed er like e needed her to stay.

"Mali," e whispered frantically, pressing their foreheads together, clutching at her clothes. "Mali, don't go. Don't. Please. I want you in my apartment, in my bed, with your fish and your hair and all your complaining about pH balances and water temperature and—"

Mali's mouth was on em again and e couldn't think of anything else.

"Yes," she whispered into er mouth. "Yes."

"But... But the bond."

"I want to bond to *you*."

Tanner couldn't stop the hungry whine that escaped er throat at that.

"That's what I was trying to tell you. A bond isn't something done lightly. I needed to know you were sure, that you wanted me living in Pebbles' kingdom forever."

"God, yes." E was so relieved, e was shaking. "Stay with me. Bond with me. I want that. All of that."

"Then take me home."

"Are you ready, little guys?" Mali whispered to the bag of fancy guppies in her arms. They must have answered back, because she giggled merrily. "I know, isn't e? I thought so, too."

"Those fish better not be sassing me. After all the work I've done for them?"

Beside Pebbles' snail kingdom stood a new, fifty-gallon tank Tanner had found on Craigslist over the weekend. It was finally ready, baby plants swaying in the water around a novelty ceramic shark.

"The fish *love* you! Now help me pour them in."

Together, they poured the contents into the water, watching the fish frantically explore their new environment.

"Welcome home, little fishies!"

Tanner pressed a kiss to her temple.

"Welcome home."

JAYLEE JAMES is a nonbinary writer, editor, and story curator native to Kansas City who is best known as the editor of *Circuits & Slippers*, an anthology of science-fiction fairytales, and *Vitality Magazine*, which published LGBTQ+ genre fiction between 2014-2016. E also writes a smattering of short fiction and video games. Learn more at JayleeJames.com.

THE DWINDLING FOREST OF KELP

by Victoria Zelvin

The translator won't translate her name. It sounds like whale song, lilting, a melody of about ten seconds that I keep trying to hum, mostly because it makes K give a trilling laugh and flip around in her tank, embarrassed and delighted, but in the end, for brevity, we agreed on K. K, for short.

The translator isn't perfect. We make it work. K is smart, so smart. She tells me she's used to conversations being a struggle across great distances with low visibility, because her people (another word that won't translate) don't live on top of one another.

Sometimes she trills. Slips about her tank, over to the corner, tucking her face into her hands. When I ask why, she tells me this is intimate. Closing curtains over it doesn't really help, because she can feel me there still. K says it's just intimate. For her people, it's like being lovers.

About a month in, I ask if that would be the worst thing.

K is smart, quick on the uptake. She responds with one of the obscene gestures I've taught her, but there's a smile splitting her face while she does it.

133

I recorded the distress message shortly after crashing and hooked it up to the escape pod's solar cells to repeat into the universe until someone came down to shut it off or the sun in this system burned out – whichever came first. It would play even after my death, provided the cells were able to retain enough power, even in blackout conditions, to clean themselves. It should play through radiation, but that's a chilling thought. What good is a distress message if I'm not sitting by the radio to answer any ships that might find it?

The message plays: *SOS. My name is Specialist Julia Marsters. I am alive and stranded on the planet. SOS. My name is Specialist Julia Marsters, and I am still alive. Please respond.*

I hear it in my nightmares.

K can only "speak" to me inside the bomber, where the translators can hear her. It's English, the standard operating system, in a monotone, robotic voice, dubbed over her lips like a kung-fu film. I imagine I look just as ridiculous to her, because sometimes she covers her mouth and trills, that laughing trill, flipping her fins at me.

She looks like a spriggan, one of those old creatures my gran told stories about before bed. Gran was of the mind that stories with monsters were far better than those without. K certainly doesn't look human. She looks hollow. She's more plant than animal, but she swims as easily as a shark. Her eyes look like little pods of bioluminescent seaweed, golden, and she's got little sparks of it all up and down her body. It's my fault she's here, trapped with me, stranded, instead of in her kelp forest. Our fault. My fault. The ships crashing from the sky are what did it, and my ship crashed too.

I wonder about the accuracy of the translator, given a hitherto unknown species, but this is what it's built for, isn't it? K and I have developed a sign language of sorts as well, though for her it is more dancing through the water than hand signs, but there's one that keeps coming up. She'll tense her whole body, hold a hand out, palm flat, fingers and fins together, frozen in the water.

"Stay," is what the bomber's AI thinks she says. It thinks she says it a lot.

The long and short of it is that I'm stranded on a planet made of water. The whole world is one big ocean, teeming with strange life. Nothing sapient, or at least that's what the reports said. I'm not sure anyone ever looked in the kelp. If they had, they would have found K.

The battle was fierce, the stuff of legends. Breathless pundits are no doubt debating it now, the merits, the loss of life, tales of tragic heroics for the human interest part, tales of those brave conscripted fighters dealing a blow to bandits and pirates haunting our borders. I doubt my contribution will be mentioned. My bomber was shot out of the stars early. It was a fluke of burning up in atmosphere that the hole in my engine, the hole that is now killing me, melted into the airtight seal that saved me.

Planet ME-07 has some continents underwater. The tumultuous sea had eroded the landmasses down to sharp chasms and trenches, but some mountain ranges remain. Close to the surface, they're home to coral reefs, small alien fish, some plant life.

K's section of the forest had surrounded one. She says she

took shelter in the coral when the sky started to fall. She thought she might've been able to swim back to her kelp when the invisible enemy started to chip away at her, started to eradicate her kelp until it was so barren that we can barely see it from our coral shelf.

I've tried to explain the word *radiation* to her, but I'm not sure she understands the why.

She understands not to surface. I understand it's because water is excellent at ionizing radiation and we're safest down here.

She understands to avoid the wreckage of ships like mine. I understand it's because the engines have cracked, protective shielding gone with the power, and they're leaking invisible poison into the water.

She understands it's safe in the bomber, the section I've flooded for her. We live half and half, her with purified water and me with my recycled air. So long as the solar panels keep up, we're okay.

She understands we're trapped. The series of ships that had crashed around us are large and powerful enough that the minefield of their leaking radiation has formed a moat around us. She didn't need much convincing of that, for all I had to show her was the line where her kelp is and the ruins of where it used to grow. A damn near perfect circle.

She understands that we're safe on the coral shelf. She understands, though, that we have to go. That our circle is shrinking. We're not safe forever. She doesn't understand why, or how, but she knows I might be able to get us there, if I can make our home float to the surface.

K wants that. She tells me, daily, hourly, that she longs for her kelp. Bits of her are flaking off. She looks sick. I believe it, I believe she needs the kelp. Either that or the radiation is affecting her more acutely than it is me. I tell her not to get near it and she spends her time lingering, fussing, trilling at me in songs I don't understand. I try to tell her my suit will protect me from low levels of radiation, warn me before I get too close to something it can't handle, but I'm not sure she entirely understands.

If I could make her a suit, enhance mine...

But, no. I delay. We have time. She's safe in here, in the bomber, in the tank. I need the bomber. If I lose the bomber, the power cells, I lose my distress signal, my radio link. I lose my ability to call out for help, even in the blind.

I lose my ticket home.

Our conversations are more complex than ever. Thank god for the universal translator. It's worth the extra lump of power, even if it is imperfect.

K tells me about her kelp. "Green," she says, animated. "Green, green, green, yellow, *green!*" I think that there's something lost in translation there, but I smile anyway. It's endearing. I've always loved to watch people talk about their passions.

"It's how I breathe," she says. She's found some plant life, perhaps the beginnings of the kelp, and has installed it in the corner of her area. I warn her not to leave her hatch open, that it might defeat the purpose of having insulation, but she just tells me that plants need light and that the window isn't enough. She swims over to her little garden often, a square-foot box of little wriggling greens, petting it as I would a cat. "It's my air. It's my air."

Does she mean it literally? She has gills. They throb even when she's not moving. Or, maybe, is she talking passion?

She's asked me what my air is, why my side of the bomber is the way it is. I say I breathe what's above the water. She flaps her hands like birds and I nod.

K lingers like a fussing mother as I swim out past our little reef. I'm wearing a suit today on top of the usual flippers and goggles. Sometimes K puts her fingers around her eyes like circles and makes fun of them, but not today. I'm venturing out into the radiation zone. With my rebreather and skintight suit, the one that covers my face like a ski mask and ensures no skin peeks through, I should be okay for a couple minutes. K had me walk her through it several times, sluggishly explaining in our bomber.

I have to get to one of the closer wrecks. It's a medical shuttle, which means it has a generator. If I can get a generator working inside the bomber, I'd be halfway to powering up the emergency flotation devices. In theory I should just have to pull a handle from the cockpit, but in practice the handle won't budge. It's probably due to something melting on entry, but regardless, I think I can power the bomber, even briefly, and surface it.

If I can do that, I can boost the power of my distress signal.

K understands, I think. Distress signal equals life. No distress signal, no life.

She still lingers. She's asked if I have a suit for her and, maybe, *maybe* the one I'm wearing would fit her, but it's the only one I've got. I don't want to risk her life on a maybe. It has to be me.

It takes hours. It's heavy and awkward and hard to grip underwater. I struggle with it most of the way back to the shelf, to the corner. K swirls around above me as I heft it, picking it up and trying to swim it up only to drop it and sending it crashing to the sand below. K suggests using the dead kelp. I bind it like rope and I help carry it from below as K pulls it up. She's distressed when I get back up. She puts her hands on me and it's like being

138

caressed by smooth seaweed, and she presses her hand over my heart and her forehead to mine for a long moment, a pregnant moment, but then she turns back to the kelp. Blackened, yellow. Brittle in the leaves, even if the stalk remains. She cradles it in her hands for a time and then tosses it to the current, like casting ashes to the wind.

It's a while before K joins me back inside. There's two hatches in the bomber, one on the bottom for me that keeps it airtight, and one on the side for her. Getting the glass up wasn't actually that hard, all things considered. Our halves aren't, strictly speaking, halves. Her half is separated not by glass but by dried gel coolant, chemically designed to be see-through. Not sure why, maybe to help steer if you happen to have a console and not an instrument panel, but either way, it makes a good enough tank.

I've got the instrument panel hooked up to the generator. The beacon is playing in the background.

SOS. My name is Specialist Julia Marsters. I am alive and stranded on the planet. SOS. My name is Specialist Julia Marsters, and I am still alive. Please respond.

"Is it making it stronger?" K asks.

"Not quite," I tell her. "I think I can make our home float. Or at least get closer to the surface. The signal is having trouble breaking through the water. That will make it stronger."

K frowns like she doesn't understand, but she doesn't ask any more questions.

It's just a normal day. I'm waiting for the generator still, so there's an itch to go back and check, but it won't be ready for a while yet. Besides, a body can't subsist on protein squares alone and K needs the sun. It's like she's fed through some kind of photosynthesis, but I'm no scientist and it won't translate. We forage together. Whenever I leave the bomber, rebreather in mouth, K is always there. I don't think I've swam without her nearby, circling me like an otter, plant-like skin fluttering behind her.

She helps me find and catch the little crabs the scanners say are safe to eat. She caresses me when she comes back to fill my net, sometimes just light, sometimes lingering long enough to put her forehead against mine.

One of these times, I catch her arm in my fingers, stopping her. I pull the rebreather from my mouth, making her scurry forward. I press my lips to hers under the water. She's salty and slimy, but the smile she gives me when it translates, when it clicks in her head, is worth it.

I blow out a series of bubbles in a laugh.

Now, when she comes back, she presses her forehead and her lips to a part of me. It makes foraging take longer, but it takes my mind off the generator.

It's becoming obvious that the translator is translating her literally.

"What's your air?" she asks, although she knows already.

"I'm not sure," I tell her. "I don't really remember."

K thinks on that for a while. It's quiet. I make dinner, if unwrapping a protein square and biting off the corner could be constituted as making dinner.

"Will there be more homes?" K asks after a while.

"Homes?"

"Homes," she repeats. She makes a gesture with her hands, putting them together with thumbs splayed out like birds.

140

"More ships, spaceships," I correct.

"Yes, homes."

It doesn't translate.

I drop my protein square back in the packaging, turning to face her, sitting cross-legged in front of the glass that separates us. "Maybe," I say. "Hopefully."

K swims back. It's like a wince. "Why want more?" The English voice is monotone, robotic, but the song sounds breathy. Afraid. Her eyes are wide.

"Working ones," I explain. "Like they're meant to be. Not dangerous, not like the wrecks. They'd be a rescue. They'd come to get me."

"Why?"

"That's... K, that's what the distress signal is."

"Distress signal... equals life?"

"Yes. Because they'd come save us. They'd get you back to the kelp, they'd get me off the planet."

K thinks about this for a time. "Why do you want to leave?"

"K, I can't stay here."

She shakes her head so emphatically that the kelpy bits of her sway like hair. She puts her hand over her chest, where my heart would be on her body. "Stay," K asks. I have to believe it's deliberate. "Stay with me."

I put my hand over my heart, massaging roughly. "It's– it's not that simple, K."

Maybe that doesn't translate either, because she's nodding. I don't think she understands.

I make K tell me the names of the sea plants growing among the coral. Outside of the bomber, it doesn't translate, but that's okay. K makes it sound like a song. I hum the words back to

141

her and she trills a laugh, nodding.

Inside, she makes me tell her the names of my plants in my apartment back on my homework. Rosemary, daffodils, aloe vera... I like a random assortment of plants, kept in different parts of the space to suit their different needs. She tries to turn those into a song too, muffled by the water.

"I'd like to see your kelp," I tell her. "Up close."

"It will love you," she assures me, tail flipping excitedly.

When I trigger the floats, K goes from inside to abruptly outside. I find her about an hour later hiding under some coral, shaking like a leaf. I caress her this time, I press my forehead to her until I coax her out, coax her back inside.

"It's not the *surface* surface," I tell her, disappointed. The bomber is not floating in the strictest sense. It is more hovering, just a bit, above the coral, but it's close enough that there's no currents strong enough to sweep it away. "But, you know, it's closer. I think the signal's boosted."

"So... more coming?" K asks, in a way that makes the robotic voice stammer.

I offer her a smile that's more like a grimace. "They might never find me here."

K smiles like this is good news.

I've only seen one other intelligent life form in months. What would I be now without K?

K is starting to brown throughout. It's like she's fading. She's gotten worse. Whole limbs that were vibrant green are now pale yellow.

I can't help but compare myself with her, in the quiet

142

moments. Sound is subdued underwater, but not thought. Am I starting to fade around the edges? How far into space does my voice reach? Have I been wasting time? Are they still looking for me? Did I miss the rescue window and now no one is coming to this side of space?

K smiles at me and it's soothing. It's only when I look away from her, it's only when she's not there, that doubt begins to wrap its thorny vines around my throat.

I try to explain to K, again, that I have to go back, that I have to help them find me, but she just asks me why again and again and I don't know how to answer the first time, let alone the twentieth. I have no family to speak of, no one to really go back to...

"Stay," K pleads with me. "We will find a way, in the kelp. They will grow to love you as I do. We can make it so you can breathe, we can figure it out. Stay."

I keep telling her it's not that simple, but K insists it is. I don't know. I just don't know.

"You need kelp," K insists. "Kelp will make it better. Trust me. It is simple. I don't want them to rot you."

God help me, I don't know. What do I really have left?

So, here's the thing. I could do it. I could do what she wants. I could get us to the kelp. The engines are too waterlogged to run, which was why I was hoping for the surface, but since that's not happening I've got one burn in them. One full cycle, enough to propel us up and then across the surface of the water like a rock skipping on a pond. One burn, we're off the coral shelf. One burn, we're in her kelp forest. I could do it.

It would cannibalize my power, though. I'd have only the solar panels for the distress beacon and so far, that hasn't been enough. I could use that one burn, that one cycle, to send my beacon up like a rocket. If I hook it up to the weapons system, angle the tube skyward... it would break atmosphere.

But then we're trapped. We're not exactly floating where we are. The bomber is too heavy, even though it is, by all accounts, technically floating. Only the top has broken the surface, and that's only sometimes.

The choice is made for me when K shuts her eyes and won't open them. Maybe it was never a choice at all. She just sort of slumps outside, the yellow encroaching on her face now. She starts to sway in the current before I swim to her, wrap my arms around her.

Maybe it was never a choice at all. Maybe it was just an illusion of a choice. I can't get back up there. I can't break atmo. I can't guarantee they're even looking for me or if getting the beacon out will bring the right kind of attention. I did what I was supposed to, I put it up. It's playing. The solar panels will keep it playing. I was fooling myself if I thought I could affect an outcome.

So I get K inside her section of the bomber. I then circle around and detach the distress beacon, one of the floats, and one solar panel. The thing floats right to the surface and bobs there, happy as can be. Transmitting. It'll keep transmitting.

There's nothing proactive I can do to help myself. I can help K, though.

That's the mantra circling my brain as I strap K into one of the side seats in her section. That's what I'm thinking when I climb into my cockpit. That's what I'm telling myself when I slam

144

the burn button and the ship slams forward.

It's the last thought in my head when my forehead hits the dash when we hit the kelp, tangling in it enough to come to a very, very sudden stop.

It's like crashing again. Waking up after, sore, trying to parse out how I am alive. There's deep bruising over my shoulders, my chest, and the bomber is at a forty-five-degree upward angle. Kelp. I'm looking up at the sun through the water, through a thick layer of kelp. We made it. When I get my bearings enough to be dizzy, I look back. The tank has broken. There's water along the back of the bomber. K's plants are hanging limply in the air, stretched back toward the water they need.

"K?" I call. I can't see her. There's no response. "K?"

There's a knock on the glass above me, enough to make me jump as the echo fades.

There, above me, is K. She's returned to green, but it's more than that. There's bioluminescent veins running through her, pulsing, glowing bright yellow. When the kelp brushes her, it lights up too, like lightning. She knocks again, giving a small wave, lips open. I hear a song then, but oh, no translator. My instruments are dead. The power's dead. Might be fixable, but to do that I'd have to leave this seat and here I am, transfixed.

K trills. Puts her hand on the glass.

I laugh then. Hysterical.

I put my hand on the other side, matching hers.

VICTORIA ZELVIN is a writer living and working in Arlington, Virginia. Her work has appeared in Daily Science Fiction, Shoreline of Infinity, and numerous anthologies. These days she is digging out from under a pile of impulse purchased unread books, and you can heckle her @victoriarius_. Her other work can be found at victoriazelvin.com.

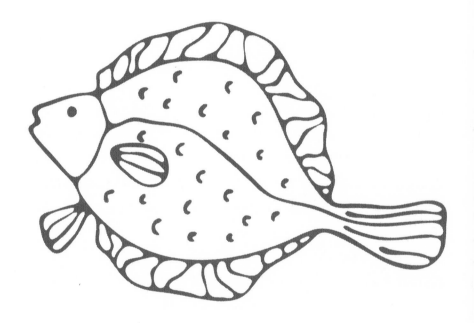

SHALLOWS

by Jennifer Lee Rossman

Two dolphins streaked through the crystal blue water, the rising sun glistening on their pink skin. They bobbed and twisted like living ripples, part of the water itself, like they used to do in the river with the rest of their pod before they were captured.

Before they became performers.

Around and around in tight circles the dolphins swam, trying to forget the burbling filters that kept the water too clean. It was the last bit of peace either of them would see that day.

One last lap. Then screaming crowds would gawk as trainers tossed them treats for their performances. One last time around the tiny pool. Then the smaller dolphin stepped out of the water.

It always felt wrong when Adriano changed. There was no pain, even as his nose shortened and his flippers turned to arms, but he hated that he had to hide his true self. He was so gangly and hairy, his skin such an odd shade of tan within any shimmer. But it meant he would see Monroe soon, and that made his heart smile.

Adriano bowed his head in reverence to the other dolphin. The park had named her Rosita, since human throats could never produce the clicks and whistles of his queen's true name. Unlike Adriano, Rosita could not change shape. Only a select few, known as *encantados*, had that ability. She returned his bow with a little head bump and a meaningless, toothy grin before swimming away.

Adriano's heart broke more with every tiny lap the dolphin queen made. He squeezed himself into his wetsuit – the mockery of a smiling cartoon whale on the back – and he reminded himself the queen would at least have a respectful trainer today.

"You're here early."

Adriano's stomach did a little flip at the voice, with its southern accent. Monroe, the sweetest, most respectful trainer at the park, whom Adriano had developed a fondness for. He scrambled to grab his floppy sun hat, and slipped on the wet tiled floor.

Into the pool he went with a splash.

The water embraced him, pulling at his soul like a magnet. This was his home, here in the depths, weightless and free. The urge to turn back into a dolphin nearly overwhelmed him, but he resisted. His tiny human lungs begged for air and he had to break the surface.

Snatching his hat off the edge of the pool and putting it snugly on his head, Adriano paddled effortlessly to the ladder and pulled himself up.

Monroe, his shirt and shoes off in preparation to dive in after him. Adriano felt that breathless pull again, seeing Monroe's concern. What a kind heart he had.

"You okay?" Monroe asked, putting a hand to Adriano's arm in concern. His skin seemed to warm at the touch. If the water couldn't hold him, this gorgeous man would be a nice substitute.

Adriano forced herself to stop staring at Monroe, stop imagining how it would feel to embrace him as a dolphin, to swim with him and rub up against his chest.

Romance was most certainly an option. For whatever

reason, Monroe found his gangly human body attractive, and made Adriano's heart sing with winks and smiles, always finding reasons to touch his arm and then pulling away shyly. He even complimented his shaved head, which was less a fashion choice and more a necessity, as even in human form, Adriano still had to breathe through a hole in his head.

Would Monroe still think he was handsome if he saw what was under the hat? He knew the answer. It was woven into every story he'd ever been told as a calf. Despite how many humans his kind had helped throughout history, lives saved from drowning, poor families shown bountiful harvests of fish in hungry times, every story ended the same way.

Rejection.

But knowing what humans thought of the encantados didn't tell him what Monroe would think. Would he paint him as a licentious, unfeeling monster, a malicious dolphin siren with cruel intentions, like the stories always said?

Could he live with Adriano's truth?

The question burned inside him, begging to be answered, but he couldn't risk it. He still needed help.

So he just smiled awkwardly. "I'm okay. I just came early because she's lonely, and the other trainers don't give her the respect she deserves." He winced as Monroe's eyes narrowed. Deep, brown eyes like a muddy river. "I don't mean you," Adriano added quickly, his cheeks turning as pink as the dolphin in the pool. "Just... She's royalty, and they have her acting like a court jester."

The analogy wouldn't make sense to Monroe. He'd never seen botos in their natural habitat, never seen the pink dolphin the park called Rosita ruling over her utopian kingdom in the waters of the Amazon.

But to his surprise, Monroe nodded. "It's wrong, keeping

149

her here." He spoke softly, his accent turning his words all twangy. His fingers trailed down Adriano's arm, leaving a wake of goosebumps. "Have you heard of..." He hesitated, didn't dare say it.

This was it, finally, the day Monroe trusted him enough to let him in on the secret Adriano had discovered months ago.

Adriano bit his lip, tried not to seem too eager. "Have I heard of what?"

"BornFree. They're an animal rights group I'm a part of, very anti-dolphinarium. Not exactly on the level, but they could help us free her..."

Adriano nodded his approval, giddy and lightheaded. It was finally happening.

They were going home.

Monroe's eyes flicked up to the security camera. "You're sure you don't want to–" He used his hand to cover his mouth so no one could read his lips, because *that* wouldn't look suspicious at all. "–go somewhere else? We could plan this at my place. The whole park layout is online." He paused, uncertain. "Or your place, or wherever. Dinner?"

Adriano froze and held his hat to his head as the wind picked up. Dinner. That was what people did on dates, wasn't it?

He stared at Monroe, mouth slightly agape. Their friendship had never been intended as anything but a way to convince him to use his connections to help free the queen. Had Adriano accidentally been flirting all along?

Human culture was so confusing.

"Do you like Italian? I make a mean lasagna."

"I... I would. Um." He couldn't very well tell Monroe that he couldn't leave the park, that his duty as the queen's footman

– or flipperman, as the case may be – bonded him to Rosita. But at the same time, declining his offer would make Adriano seem disinterested, and he was anything but.

Monroe waited patiently, letting the current of noisy tourists flow around them.

"We should focus on the heist for now," Adriano finally said.

If Monroe was disappointed, he didn't let it show, still smiling that smile that made Adriano go all gooey inside. "We should probably not call it a heist in front of all these witnesses."

"They aren't paying attention," Adriano pointed out. Humans never did, or else they would have noticed by now that it was wrong to take an animal that once had all the water in the world and put it in a little bowl.

"There she is," Monroe said, pointing to someone in the crowd. His contact from BornFree, a woman named Carly who would help them coordinate the rescue.

Funny. Adriano had dreamed of going home for so long, dreamed of shedding the awkward human form and frolicking through the river for the rest of his days. But now that it was real and everything was happening so fast, his stomach clenched a little at the thought.

He didn't have a mate back home. Friends and family, yes, and he loved them more than anything, but a mate was different. Not better, not more important, just a different kind of love he hadn't known he'd wanted until now.

Monroe caught him staring and Adriano dropped his gaze to the ground, his cheeks turning pink as a river dolphin.

The orca flung itself into the air, coming down with a thunderous splash that sent a tidal wave over the shrieking front rows of the audience.

Adriano flinched as the chilly water hit him. It took more than a few drops to trigger his turn, but his body ached at the sensation trickling down his skin, the water molecules pulling at his shapeshifter magic.

Monroe touched his arm. "You okay?" he whispered.

He was not. Adriano had never seen the show from the outside, never seen the grinning, overeager trainer prattling on about the majesty of the creatures they were imprisoning. Is that what he looked like? Did people think he *enjoyed* making Rosita dance for fish?

But Adriano couldn't tell Monroe any of that, because the human boy had the sort of smile that made you feel safe enough to tell all your secrets. If Adriano started opening up, he feared he wouldn't be able to stop himself. Instead, Adriano just shrugged and leaned on Monroe's shoulder.

The three of them – Adriano, Monroe, and his friend Carly – were the only guests not cheering wildly as the orca twirled and dove for treats. They were here for reconnaissance.

"These three show tanks are centrally located," Carly whispered, making notes on a souvenir map from the gift shop. "It would be quicker to drive a crane up to this auditorium than have to go around to all of their holding tanks."

"We can get them to the show tanks," Monroe said confidently. "Just give us a week or two to figure out the timing, map all the blind spots in the security system."

A week or two? Adriano looked up at Monroe. That didn't feel like very much time anymore.

In the darkened building where they housed the exotic fish, Adriano and Monroe stood shoulder-to-shoulder over

Carly's map of the zoo.

It wasn't just Rosita and the orcas. Monroe wanted to free everyone — even the seals and otters. *His heart must be bigger than any other human's,* Adriano mused, and told himself that was why he liked to stare at his chest: to see if he could see how just how large.

Not because Monroe wore shirts so thin and tight that Adriano could see every carved muscle.

Nope, definitely not.

He wondered what Monroe would say if he knew the truth. That Adriano was bonded to the other dolphin and couldn't leave, that he that he sprouted a tail and flippers every night to swim with his queen.

Would Monroe still like him if he knew?

"So..." Monroe chewed his lip in thought, scribbling idly on the margins of the map. "We've got about eight hours where no one is here, yeah? And thirty animals to move?"

"The otters and seals will be easy," Adriano pointed out. "They're trained to follow people. After that it's just three bottlenose, five orcas, and the boto."

Monroe nodded, and his lip went further into his mouth. Adriano unconsciously mimicked him. In the dim blue glow of the piranha tank, he could almost imagine they were underwater, Monroe's dark hair floating gracefully around his face.

"We'll have to figure out how long it takes to load each one. After that, it's just a math problem." Monroe flashed Adriano a smile that melted his insides. "'If Monroe and Adriano have nine cetaceans and three cranes, and it takes an hour to load each one, how much time will their heist-slash-rescue take?'"

Having never been to school or taken a math test, Adriano wasn't entirely sure why he phrased it that way. But it made Monroe laugh, and that was a glorious sound. This soft-hearted,

153

human boy's very presence pulled at him, the way he thought only water could.

Adriano wanted to fall into him.

The truth of what he was echoed loudly in Adriano's skull, begging to be spoken. But he couldn't risk it, not while he still needed Monroe and his friends to get home.

"We still have the transport tanks from when we brought them in," Monroe continued, looking more at Adriano than at the plans. "So we can get those on trucks the night before, fill them secretly during the day, then it's just a matter of getting the animals in and getting the trucks to BornFree. And then they're off to natural habitats, or at least bigger facilities. Ones with open-ocean pens, where they don't have to perform."

He worried his lip again. Transporting aquatic mammals was stressful and often dangerous.

"It'll be okay." Adriano put his hand on his shoulder, and suddenly their lips were pressed together. Just a quick kiss, but charged with electricity. It left Adriano with the kind of exhilaration he had only ever felt while swimming.

Adriano longed for more. Not just physical contact, but going on dates and sharing a life together. Maybe sharing secrets, too.

"I'm putting all of my trust in you," Monroe whispered. "My partner in crime."

Adriano wanted to return the sentiment but he couldn't. Not right now.

He broke contact, feeling himself growing heavy again.

Plastic seals and whales stared down at them from atop gaudy signs advertising ice cream and soda pop. Even in the moonlight, their bright colors and cheerful grins made a mockery of the noble creatures they represented.

"We are so dead," Monroe muttered.

Adriano knelt in the shallow end with his queen, using all of his concentration to remain in his human form while he watched Monroe pace on the trainer deck. Every so often, Monroe would dash off and shout commands to Carly and the others, only to return to the pink dolphin pool with his nervous energy.

"We aren't dead," Adriano soothed, running his hands over the dolphin's back. The animal struggled against the sling suspending her in the water, squeaking and chirping in a language Adriano couldn't understand in his current form.

The two most important people in his life were in distress. Adriano didn't know if his heart could handle this much longer. He shushed Rosita, pressing a kiss to her thrashing head, and cooed an old Brazilian lullaby.

"We might not be dead, but..." Monroe indicated the dolphin.

Though he didn't say it outright, Adriano knew he was thinking of his and Rosita's first day at the park the year before. A pair of dolphins were taken from the Amazon, but only one survived the trip. The youngest died from the stress.

At least, that was what Adriano had told them when they found him in the truck wearing stolen clothes and a woman's sunhat too big for his head. He couldn't just come out and say he had transformed into a man during transit to better watch over his queen.

"And the cops are on their way," Monroe said.

"You don't know that."

He gestured to the long neck of the crane reaching over the pool, and the others like it jutting up across the park. "We're not exactly being subtle, darling."

Darling.

155

It was just his southern upbringing. He probably called a lot of people darling.

But it still made Adriano feel like he was floating.

"We're going to get caught. And do you know how many laws we're breaking? Because it isn't just the theft of endangered species. It's stolen trucks and cranes and forged travel documents and–"

"Come here." Adriano patted the water beside him.

"I don't have time–"

"Just come here for a second."

Monroe stripped off his shoes and socks and waded in. Their legs brushed against each other.

"Do you feel it?"

Monroe furrowed his brow.

"The water." Adriano gave himself to the pool, floating on his back. His queen squealed, slapping the surface with her head. Adriano heard every ripple hit his body, a foreign language slipping away every time he tried to grasp it.

Monroe came down with a heavy splash beside him, doubt lining his face.

Dolphin and the promise of home on one side, and on the other, human and the chance to feed the hunger in his heart. Both pulled at Adriano so hard he thought he might tear in half.

Did he really have to go back to the river with his queen? Could he break his bond, give up the deep and walk forever on land?

Why did he have to decide?

"You guys ready?" Carly called out from above.

No, Adriano thought desperately. I'm not.

But Monroe shouted, "Yeah!" and the crane hoisted the sling. Water poured down in tearful splatters as the pink dolphin queen was lifted away.

Adriano got up to go after her, pulling himself from the calm of the water, but Monroe put a hand to his cheek. His lips were soft, so unbelievable soft, moving in slow waves with passion and the relief of knowing the last animal was on its way to safety.

In that moment, Monroe's pull was stronger than anything else. Adriano ceased to feel the water or hear the chaos around him.

There was only the echolocation of their heartbeats, the touch of Monroe's hand moving across his back.

Adriano sank into the kiss, letting go of everything else. Only when he started to understand snippets of Rosita's distant squeaks did he realize his mistake.

He was turning.

He felt his skin grow slick, his ankles snap together to form a tail, and tried to fight it. But it was too late.

The kiss froze, Monroe's lips tight and his eyes wide in horror. He'd felt the slick, rubbery skin.

He pushed away from Adriano. "What are you?"

Adriano wanted to dissolve. To break apart and become part of the water. Anything to stop seeing the shock – and was that disgust? – on Monroe's face. Grabbing his hat, he dashed after Rosita. He thought he heard Monroe calling after him, but didn't look back.

"I thought there was only one."

"And where's the guy that was with her?"

Water muffled the human voices, turning them garbled and distant as the men peered into the tanks.

The truck had passed through many hands, all of them allies of Monroe and Carly. At each border crossing, Adriano had been in the back, singing calming songs to his queen and presenting false paperwork, praying they wouldn't be found out. But during the long stretches of driving, he had slipped into the tank and turned back to his natural state.

News had come over the radio early in the morning. All the mammals at Seaside Dolphinarium and Amusement Park were missing, along with two of their trainers.

Adriano's heart ached at his foolishness. Falling for a human who could never love him. Not the *real* him, the encantado shapeshifter.

Monroe was the land itself. Tempting and beautiful, but at the same time inhospitable. Deceiving. He welcomed Adriano, drew him in with promises that turned empty as soon as he dared let himself feel safe. Adriano hadn't even seen him since the night of the heist, since the disastrous kiss. He figured Monroe had gone with one of the other trucks, all the better to avoid the freaky dolphin boy.

Monroe was human, and humans only loved things on their terms. They saw a pink dolphin, and they had to own it, make it perform. Adriano had thought he could fall into that world, but there was no depth to be found. Only shallowness and smiling plastic whales.

Through the open door of the container truck came a humid breeze that smelled of jungle flowers and... and river water.

Adriano and his queen sang out, their home calling to them. He could hear the other dolphins, understand them. The pull was so great, it almost hurt.

But when they lifted the dolphins out of the tank, and he saw the Amazon ribboning its way through the rainforest, he felt another pull in the opposite direction. He turned his agile neck and saw not one truck, but two.

A dizzy lightness came over him. Had Monroe came with them after all?

The two dolphins slipped into the water. Cool and silty. Home.

It welcomed him like a lost child, but Monroe's voice called to him. Adriano saw to it that his queen was safe with the other dolphins, then went to the surface. He felt his tail split into legs, his face shorten.

It felt wrong. The water tugged at him, tempting him back into the deep. But there was Monroe, kneeling on the shore, waiting to take Adriano's hands in his.

"I'm sorry," he said. "It just surprised me is all. Not every day your crush turns into a beautiful pink dolphin." There was that smile that made Adriano's heart sing. "I should have come back to check on you, but I wasn't sure you'd want to see me, so I stayed in the cab. But I can't stop thinking about you and I just want you to know my offer of lasagna still stands. Or... um, maybe sushi would be more appropriate?"

"I can't leave them," Adriano said. "They're my family, and their love is everything to me."

"When did I ask you to leave them?"

Adriano dropped his voice to a shameful whisper. "I'm a dolphin."

"And I'm a fugitive."

Their kiss was a bridge between worlds, and all was in balance. The pull of land and water, equalized in the shallows.

JENNIFER LEE ROSSMAN is a science fiction geek from Oneonta, New York, who has never ever threatened to run over anyone with her wheelchair. Nope, definitely not. Her debut novel, *Jack Jetstark's Intergalactic Freakshow*, will be published in December. She blogs at jenniferleerossman.blogspot.com and tweets @JenLRossman.

SIGNING UNDER THE SEA

by Lizzie Colt

After a long day of swimming in the deep, Seaweed is exhausted and goes to rest on the rocks. Her kind usually congregates there, but Seaweed is alone for now and she takes the opportunity to stretch her leg. Her right leg – now her only leg – gets tired so easily since she lost the other one in a net.

She hates how humans discard everything in her ocean. And now they even lived under the sea in big, glass domes. They made a treaty with the leader of the ocean people, saying they will clean up and undo the damage to the sea if they are left in peace to do their science.

Seaweed doesn't know what to think. It's because of humans she went through great pain and now struggles to swim with only one webbed foot, if they keep their word, their being here might mean no other ocean folk has to go through what she went through. The days of agony are tattooed onto her memory, a pain she'll never forget.

All of a sudden, she's snapped out of her thoughts when she spots her ocean sister swimming fast toward her. Seaweed takes a moment, echoes of pain still in her mind and bones. "Shell,

161

what is it? Is something wrong?"

"Nothing is wrong. I've seen something amazing!" Shell flips over in the water, clearly excited.

"What?" Seaweed hopes her young sister hasn't met another boy. She doesn't seem to get that no men interest Seaweed, not ocean folk men, not mermen or selkie men, and certainly not human men.

"There is a human who speaks with their hands, like that sailor you told me about." Shell beams.

Eli is the only human Seaweed has ever had positive contact with. He gave her fish when she first lost her leg and had trouble hunting, not as fast then as she is now. He had no voice, not like the other humans Seaweed had heard yelling aboard their ships, and not like ocean folk who spoke with voices like human music. Instead, he signed with his hands, and had tried to teach her. It fascinated Seaweed. She felt like he understood what it was like to be missing something everyone else had.

He left when the weather changed, and had not returned. He showed her an image of other humans; his family, she was sure. Seaweed knows humans live together just like ocean folk but on land in stone shelters, and hopes he's happy wherever he is.

"Was it a man?" Seaweed asks, hoping that maybe her friend has returned.

Shell frowns. "I don't know. They had long hair tied up, but a flat chest. They looked like both kinds of human."

The sailor was a human male, so this news disappoints Seaweed. She didn't know that humans, like ocean folk, had more than two genders. Maybe there's more to humans than she knows, more than nets and fish.

"Where are they?" Seaweed asks.

"Out on the ocean floor, around the dome, in those strange

suits they wear." Shell wrinkles her face in confusion. She's never understood why humans can only breathe above the surface, with all their technology surely, they could change themselves.

"Doing what?" Seaweed knows the ocean is dangerous for humans and wonders what could be worth the risk.

Shell darts closer to her sister and sits on a bit of wreckage. "A group of them are cleaning,"

Cleaning, like they promised?

"I'm going to look!"

"Can I come?"

"No, go to Father. Tell him and the elders where I have gone, so you can come for me if I don't return by tomorrow." Seaweed is no fool. She won't risk her ocean sister and won't let her own curiosity put her in too much danger. At the very least, the elders will see her avenged if she's harmed.

"But I found the human!"

"Don't argue with me, Shell. You know I can still beat you in a fight." Seaweed bares her sharp teeth, though she has no urge to hurt Shell. She doesn't want to explain why she's fearful for her, but taking the risk herself, because she hardly understands her reason.

Shell sighs but nods, and Seaweed heads for the domes, they are large glass and metal structures with portals showing into labs and living quarters. When they finally come into sight, Seaweed sees the humans. She hides behind some debris and watches.

There are five humans, and four of them keep pressing buttons on the arm of their suits, making noise. But one does not, and Seaweed focuses on them. They do look androgynous, and beautiful for a human, their white skin so much less interesting than the shades of blue the ocean folk's skin comes in They look more like the merfolk. Well, the top half of merfolk, anyway.

Seaweed waits and observes. Eventually the human she's interested in gestures with their hand and moves away from the group. Seaweed follows the human to an entrance into the dome, and when they open a small door, Seaweed darts past and into a small, still underwater space. The human looks surprised but doesn't draw a weapon, just shuts the door.

The human raises their hands and makes a sign, then points to a button, asking if the water can be drained in sign. Seaweed nods. The human presses the button. Once the water level is below their heads, the human takes off their helmet.

Seaweed signs hello and then fingerspells her name. The human's angular face lights up, and they sign back that their name is Dee. Then the human asks if Seaweed is deaf, and Seaweed shakes her head. By then, all the water is gone and the air feels strange on her skin, and the human strips off their bulky suit, revealing a slim frame. Seaweed doesn't know much about humans, but she'd like to know more, so she asks in sign if she can talk with Dee.

Dee looks excited and takes something out of her pocket. Seaweed is nervous and ready to defend herself, despite needing to lean against the wall to help her leg support her weight without the water's buoyancy. If Dee means her harm, Seaweed will go down fighting. But Dee doesn't attack; They offer Seaweed a small device that looks like what humans call a cellphone. Seaweed thought those didn't work under the sea. When Seaweed doesn't take it right away, Dee types something on the device.

This machine can talk for me, but it also texts. I have another. If you want to talk, we can use this.

The robotic voice is strange, but Seaweed takes the offered device and puts it in the small pouch she wears around her waist.

Seaweed signs that her leg is getting tired; Dee looks worried and quickly presses more buttons on the keypad. A bench slides

164

out of the wall, and Seaweed sits gratefully. When she swims, her missing leg is not much of an issue, but on land, she feels more pain if she has to stand for very long without support.

Dee sits down, too, and they both look at each other, neither hiding their curiosity. Dee signs ocean folk", and Seaweed nods, pleased that Dee knows her species. So many mistake her for a mermaid, despite her lack of tail.

Seaweed knows she shouldn't stay long, not knowing more about the humans inside the dome who could be dangerous, and she signs that she must go. Dee frowns and asks if Seaweed will message her and maybe come back. Seaweed nods, and Dee stands, putting her suit back on. Water fills the tunnel again, and Dee lets them out into the ocean.

Swimming feels far more natural than standing had, and she wonders what humans do if they lose a leg. Maybe they have some kind of device, like Dee and the talking cell phone. Once outside, Dee signs that it was nice to meet her, and Seaweed agrees and says goodbye, swimming off before she can do anything foolish like make an embarrassing mistake in front of Dee

She tries to put the pretty human out of her mind, but by the time she's in the underground caves where the ocean folk live, ready to sleep, she finds herself lying with the cellphone-like object in her hands. It takes a few tries to get it to light up, and then she finds Dee's name listed with others and copies what she's seen the sailor do. He called it a *text*.

Not sure what to send, Seaweed starts simple, saying hello and reminding Dee who she is.

Dee replies that she's glad to be in contact, and they start talking. Seaweed is surprised how easy the human is to talk to, easier even than Shell or the rest of her family. She thinks maybe Dee knows what it's like to be different, not being able to talk to the other humans in the same way. Seaweed's family does their

165

best, but they don't understand her pain or the way every action takes so much effort.

> S: Why did you come to the ocean?
> D: I love the sea... it's so beautiful, and down here people judge me less, they're willing to talk with me the way I communicate
> S: Don't all humans sign?
> D: No, a lot don't even try to talk to me in ways I can understand. Some just yell at me, and they don't seem to understand that doesn't help. How did you learn human sign?
> S: A sailor taught me. I miss him

Seaweed is surprised by her own confession, but there is something about talking this way that makes her feel less intimidated than being face-to-face with a person, ocean folk included.

> D: Was he a lover of a friend? Wait, is that too personal to ask? I'm bad at being social
> S: He was a friend. I don't take cis male lovers
> D: I miss some of my friends from on land. I hope maybe we can be friends
> S: I hope so, too

They text all night, until Seaweed falls asleep. When she wakes, a message waits for her.

D: Do you have a family?

S: A big one: three younger sisters, many aunts and uncles and cousins, my parents, too. Do you?

D: I have parents and a brother but they live on land. It's been months since I saw them

S: Do you feel lonely?

D: Sometimes

S: Me too, even with my family close. I'm not like them, wasn't even before I lost my leg

D: It can be hard being different from those around you, even if you love them, even if they love you

S: I agree. The ocean feels so big and empty at times, like I'm the only one like me down here

D: I think I understand that feeling; I feel it on land too

S: I'm glad you came to the ocean

D: I'm glad too. I have to go do some work, but can I message you again tonight?

S: Yes, I'd like that

They say their goodbyes and Seaweed finds herself waiting for Dee to message her all day even though she knows she has hours to wait. She spends the time with her sisters, who are full of questions but don't push her too far, knowing they owe their eldest sister respect, and that she's been in more fights than all three of them combined. There are many in the ocean who prey on her because of her missing leg, thinking she won't fight back.

When Dee finally messages her, Seaweed asks if Dee has ever had to fight others because of her hearing.

D: Not physically, but I often need to fight for respect, to not be treated like a child

S: I'm sorry, I would fight them for you

D: Thank you, I have to sleep now, but please message again

S: How was work?

D: Great, I was in the lab today, looking at how things grow

S: You love your job, don't you?

D: Yes, so much. I want to fix what humans have done to the ocean, to clean it and let it grow the way it's meant to. You told me your job is hunting and caring for younger ocean folk, do you like that?

S: Sometimes. Hunting is necessary but boring. Young ocean folk can be fun; they're all so different

They talk more about their jobs and kids, and Seaweed is surprised how similar human children are to ocean folk young. Dee shares a goal of having lots of children in their life one day. Seaweed wants the same, as she has grown up with lots of young and does desire her own even though some people thinks she should not have them; she is shocked to find out some humans don't think Dee should be a parent because they're deaf.

As each day passes, they talk more and more deeply. Dee tells Seaweed about growing up on land, being deaf, and how things like going to the movies had been different for her to the other kids. It sounds difficult, but Seaweed likes the idea of movies. Dee says maybe they can watch one together in the dome.

Seaweed keeps the nature of her new friendship secret

from her family. It feels too fragile, like a sea flower, like anything could come along and destroy it, and Seaweed wants it to survive. She finds herself always excited for Dee's messages She talks about how she's felt since losing her leg, emotions she's never felt she could share with her family, so afraid they'll pity her, but Dee doesn't do that ever and Seaweed knows in her heart Dee won't because she's been faced with pity herself and it's left the same bitter taste in her mouth.

Seaweed isn't sure when exactly she falls in love with Dee, but she is sure that's what this feeling is. Her heart races every time she gets a message from Dee, still excited even if Dee is just asking a simple question, like what she likes to eat or what it's like to swim under the sea without any aids.

Dee seems to care about every detail of Seaweed's day, nothing is too small or boring. And Dee shares herself, answering everything Seaweed asks about Dee's life and the human world.

When Dee asks her to come to the tunnel again, Seaweed is nervous, but she says yes.

Seaweed tells Shell where she's going, and makes her promise not to tell anyone else unless she is gone after the next sunrise. Shell doesn't understand why Seaweed wants to go back again, but Seaweed dares not explain that Dee's words have captured something inside of her. She swims to the dome and finds the right door. Dee is waiting and lets Seaweed in and drains the water, the bench ready for Seaweed.

I have a gift for you. So you can walk on land and inside the dome.

Dee uses her device to speak, and then picks up a long stick with a handle off the floor. Seaweed accepts the gif and takes a step. It's a little awkward, but far better than without the stick.

Dee must have remembered what Seaweed told her about missing walking on the beach. Happiness swells up inside Seaweed at the thoughtfulness, and she hugs Dee on instinct.

Dee seems surprised but hugs her back.

Maybe I can show you around the dome sometime.

Seaweed signs, asking if that's allowed, and Dee nods. They sit together for hours this time, talking about their lives, their families, the world above the ocean that Dee has lived in and Seaweed talks about life beneath the waves, the different creatures and clans. When Dee needs to go, Seaweed is sad, and Dee seems to feel the same.

Will you come back?

Seaweed nods, and then, summoning up all of her courage, asks if she can kiss Dee.

Dee looks thrilled, her smile bright, and nods.

Seaweed touches Dee's face and kisses her gently. Her heart tells her this will be the first of many.

The ocean is deep and full of many mysterious things, but one mystery Seaweed hasn't experienced is love. Who'd have thought a human would change that?

LIZZIE COLT is a disabled, bisexual writer in her mid-twenties, who is trying to break into the world of YA and other kinds of romance. She also writes erotica under the pen name L.J. Hamlin. You can find Lizzie at @lizziecolt or @ljhamlin and at ljhamlin.com.

ONDINE

by M. Hollis

The cab door closed, and the driver drove off in a hurry, leaving Serena alone in front of her childhood home for the first time in eight years.

Everything looked the same as she remembered, although a bit older and dustier. The front lawn was overgrown, and spiderwebs were starting to form around the front balcony. Her mother had probably been too weak to look after the place in her final years.

It was so strange to think her mother was gone. She had seemed so young but a heart attack at fifty-five was like that – abrupt and sudden. Serena had received a call in the middle of the night, boarded a plane, and now she was here.

The flight back to Santa Helena Island took twenty hours. She hated that she had missed the funeral.

When Serena turned nineteen, she had gone as far away as she could. At the time, escaping from family obligations and this damned small island had felt like the best thing in the world. She had dedicated her life to a career in journalism, thinking she would have the entire world at her feet if she could just get away from her childhood home.

But now, walking around this tiny house, finding her mother's quilt still on her favorite chair, Serena was full of regrets.

She thought they'd have more time. But eight years had passed, and they didn't even get to say goodbye.

Serena touched every surface as if committing to memory all the things she remembered from this house. The chipped coffee table, the cupboard filled with old family heirlooms, and the pictures on the walls. She smiled at a photo of the two of them together. Serena was seven or eight years old, grinning as she held up a big fish she caught, her mother laughing by her side.

All lost in the past.

Her mother's books were on display on the bookshelves, most of them stories about the beings that lived in the seas and oceans. People called it fiction, gave her mother literature awards, and called her an imaginative, creative soul.

Serena was a writer, too, but had taken a different path than her mother. While her mother had preserved the tales of the ocean, Serena wrote about the truth behind the stories in the news.

Serena sighed heavily and decided she needed a bath before she did anything else. After cleaning herself and leaving her bag in her old bedroom, she went downstairs to commence sorting her mother's things.

The sound of someone walking around the kitchen made her stop in her tracks. She had thought the house was empty. Who could it be?

Serena took cautious steps towards the door, her heart jumping inside her chest. What if a burglar had come in? But when she looked inside the room, she found only a young woman going through the cupboards.

"Excuse me?" Serena asked.

The woman turned around, and Serena's eyes widened. It was one of *them*, no doubt. Long green hair, slightly grey skin, and that inhuman aura that always surrounded them. Serena could feel their connection, a thread pulsing through her veins like an old song long forgotten. She had managed to hide it from herself for years, but it was still there somehow.

"Sorry, did I scare you?" the woman asked.

Serena shook her head. "I just wasn't expecting to see someone here."

The woman nodded. "I'm sorry. I'm Ylsa. Your mother was my mentor in her remaining years and in return, I looked after her as best as I could." Ylsa smiled and went back to the cupboard. "Do you want a coffee? Must have been a long trip."

"Yes, please," Serena said, calmer now.

She sat down at the small kitchen table, watching as Ylsa moved things around as if she belonged there. It was a strange scene. She seemed more at home than Serena. When Ylsa turned around, she brought the two cups of coffee to the table and sat across from Serena.

Ylsa took a sip of her coffee and hummed in contentment, a sound that brought a glint of memory to Serena's mind. She frowned, trying to remember what it was about the noise that seemed so familiar.

"Do I know you?" she asked.

Ylsa looked up, her green eyes so vivid now. "You do."

Something clicked inside Serena's mind and she recognized Ylsa.

"The little girl who always came over," Serena said in a whisper.

Ylsa nodded.

The memories came flooding back to Serena. Waking up one morning to see a little girl with green hair crying in the living room, Serena's mother trying to soothe her. Ylsa had been lost, swimming around their beach without finding her way back home. Serena's mother had taken care of her that day, and at

173

night, Serena and Ylsa had slept together in Serena's tiny bed.

There was something about Ylsa that had entranced Serena. It was similar to the connection she had to their people, but still entirely different somehow. Something she had never felt with anyone else before. She knew the bond between her and her mother as family, but Ylsa was a part of her that was still fresh and unknown, her skin so soft against Serena's as they fell asleep.

Over the years, Ylsa was a regular visitor. They'd built sandcastles and proclaimed themselves the queens of Santa Helena, hid underwater, and ate Serena's mother's strawberry cake at the end of every day.

"You stopped coming," Serena said.

"I did." There was sadness in Ylsa's eyes. "You were angry. I thought you hated all of us."

Serena took a sip of coffee, guilt filling her. In her teenage years, she rebelled against their nature. She had been confused and trapped between two worlds where she could never really belong. Her mother forbade her from telling her human friends about the creatures that dwelt in the sea, and Serena couldn't see herself leaving humans behind to live beneath the waves.

"I'm sorry. It wasn't you, I was just..."

"Lost," Ylsa finished for her.

"Yes."

They stayed in silence for a few minutes. The sound of the ocean outside brought shivers to Serena's skin. Seeing Ylsa here, back in her kitchen after so many years, gave her some perspective on everything she had lost.

"After you were gone..." Ylsa said. "Your mother was sad. She rarely came to see us down under. Everyone was worried, and I decided to come visit once in a while."

"I've been a terrible daughter," Serena said, laughing sadly.

Ylsa moved closer, her fingers closing around Serena's. She

was cold, a stark reminder of her otherworldly nature. "That's not true. We all need to find our place in the world."

Serena had been underwhelmed with what the human world had offered her. She had never felt like she belonged, yet couldn't put into words what she was searching for. The world was cruel and harsh, and she couldn't connect with anyone, not the way she felt the connection with her people.

"I was a terrible friend too," Ylva said. She looked down, a sad smile growing on her face.

Was she thinking the same things Serena was?

"Do you remember the last time we saw each other?" Ylsa asked.

Serena brushed a finger on her forehead. She did. She remembered it clearly. The soft rain falling on the beach, Ylsa's hair tied in a low braid, her eyes watery with the tears she refused to shed. Both of their lips still tingling from that first ardent kiss.

"I'm sorry," Serena said. "I shouldn't have left things like that. I shouldn't have said those things."

Serena shook her head, trying to get rid of the foggy memories.

I hate the sea. I hate this island. There is no way I'll stay stuck in this place forever.

She knew how much this must have hurt Ylsa.

"I understand if you can't forgive me."

Ylsa's forehead furrowed. She tightened her grip on Serena's hand, the bond flowing between them stronger than ever.

"I won't lie. It hurt. And it took me a long time to understand your point of view. But it's in the past now. You came back. Shouldn't that matter?"

Serena nodded weakly, her resolve still uncertain.

"I was young too," Ylsa said. "It's not like I tried to help.

175

You ran to the mainland, I ran to the sea. Both of us were just kids."

The silence stretched between them for a few minutes. Serena felt a shift in the air, her shoulders relaxing slightly.

"What are you going to do now?" Ylsa asked. "Your mother needs to be honored."

Serena's mother had been the guardian of the Inbetween for thirty years. She had taken care of the beach, hiding their secrets from the invaders who came around, and providing safety for the sea creatures who were curious about dry land. Now that she was gone, she had to be honored in the waters and replaced by someone else. Ylsa would be a perfect choice. She had been there all this time. But if Serena left, would Ylsa be able to do the work by herself?

"I'm not sure," Serena said.

"Either way, you have to go back. At least once. They are waiting for you. They have been waiting for you for a long time now," Ylsa said.

"I know."

They finished their coffee and walked to the beach. The moon was full, and the sand was cold under their bare feet.

Serena could feel her mother's soul in everything. She was in the air that breathed on Serena's face, in the seashells on the ground.

Ahead of them, the waves broke again and again and again. The cycle that never ended.

Serena hesitated a few steps before the waves. The beach was still the same after all these years. Her childhood home, the place she knew as her own. But *she* had changed. Would she remember the ways of the sea again?

"Are you okay?" Ylsa asked, standing by her side.

"I'm terrified."

With slow movements, Ylsa walked until she was in front of Serena. Her eyes were so full of gentleness and something else Serena couldn't put her finger on. Ylsa placed a hand on Serena's shoulder and heart.

"This is your place in this world," Ylsa said. "Take it back. I'll be here for you this time. No running away. But you have to stop running away, too."

Serena's heart jumped a beat. She could feel herself letting go, a part of her reaching out to the sea now, begging her to touch the water. And then there was Ylsa. Beautiful, gentle Ylsa who took care of her mother all these years Serena wasn't there. Ylsa who had loved her.

Ylsa who she let go a long time ago because they weren't ready for this.

Maybe it was time to try again. Time for Serena to find the happiness she had been running away from.

"I'm ready," she said.

Ylsa gave her a small smile and moved forward, placing a chaste kiss on the other girl's cheek. Serena closed her eyes. Just that soft touch already brought so many tumultuous feelings, filling her with hope and dreams for the two of them. When she opened her eyes again, Ylsa was already steps ahead of her.

She followed Ylsa to the jetty. The only sound was the waves and their shoes against the wood. Ylsa slowly got rid of her clothes, showing off her pale grey skin. She dove into the water and looked back at Serena, beckoning her to follow. Serena stared at the distant ocean ahead of her. It had been so long since she last did this.

She took off her clothes and climbed down the steps until she was completely submerged. As her sight became accustomed to the darkness, she watched in fascination as Ylsa changed shape before her.

A prickling sensation in Serena's hands signaled the beginning of her own transformation. Her fingers became webbed as they grew longer and thinner. Her feet lengthened, webbing developing between her toes as her whole body became sleeker and more powerful. Finally, her nose shrunk and vanished, replaced by gills on either side of her neck. She gave Ylsa a nod, and they dove into the depths.

It was easy from then on. The pulsing was back in Serena's bones, guiding her way through the ocean like a tide she couldn't fight against. The deeper she swam, the higher her soul soared. The Ondines were all connected, no matter if they were dead or alive. The connection would live through generations yet to come, reminding them to always come back home.

Serena had been ignoring that calling from the ocean that lived inside her soul for a long time, learning how to stop listening to the songs from her people she still knew in her heart. But being underwater, following Ylsa to the place where her people made their home, left her overwhelmed. No other place made her feel like this.

As a teenager, this had scared her. Her school friends were moving away, growing up, finding new places and people. Serena had nowhere but the sea. But the call from the ocean made her fear that she'd lose the humanity she had inherited from her father. The father who had abandoned Serena and her mother when Serena was still a baby.

Ylsa swam over to a rock formation on the ocean floor, finding a fissure and dipping inside. As soon as Serena followed her into the cavern, she felt the presence of the others waiting for them.

Deep in the darkness, under the sea, the Ondines lived in a cavern so big that one could get lost inside. Many humans had, despite the Ondines warning.

Dozens of Ondines lived in this cavern, each with similar long green hair and webbed fingers like Ylsa's. Many more found homes in different oceans of the world. Their eyes were used to the dark, but the rocks where they slept were covered in seaweed that shone in bioluminescent tones of pink, purple, green, and yellow. The sudden brightness in the cavern and the presence of the other Ondines was too much for Serena.

She wanted to weep, but the only sound she was capable of was a sad lament which reverberated around the cavern. The others came closer, taking turns to embrace her. All of them felt Serena's mother's death with her in that moment and mourned the loss of one of their own.

They began to sing, loud and clear. Ancient words the Ondine sang to every new generation from the moment they were born. Serena closed her eyes and let the song flow through her. She wanted to cherish this new communion she felt with her own kind.

When she opened her eyes again, Ylsa was by her side, green eyes concerned.

Serena could see it then, their future. Ylsa and Serena growing old together. One on land, another in the ocean. They'd take care of the Inbetween, bring new children to this world, and learn to love the place they protected.

Serena had been wrong before. She didn't need to go anywhere to find herself. She was right here. In between the waves, in Ylsa's eyes, and in the songs of their people.

Ylsa offered her a hand, swimming closer and closer. Serena let her childhood friend embrace her, the cold skin bringing fireworks to every inch of her body. She still had a human instinct to return to the land.

But this was how it should be.

She would learn to be one with the water again. In the end,

there was nowhere else she'd prefer to be. Serena followed Ylsa to the middle of the circle the others were forming, and they danced and sang together, honoring her mother so that her spirit could rest in the hearts of her people, and in the heart of her daughter who would now take her place.

M. HOLLIS could never decide what to do with her life. Since childhood, she has changed her mind hundreds of times, but decided to fully dedicate herself to her stories. When she isn't blogging at bibliosapphic.wordpress.com, tweeting @_mhollis, or reading lots of femslash fanfiction, you'll find her crying about female characters and baking cookies.

ACKNOWLEDGMENTS

JAYLEE JAMES

An anthology is nothing without the authors writing the stories to go in it. And this one would also be nothing without my tireless co-editor, Jennifer, who was willing to take on work when we struggled with delay after delay.

I'm so thankful to everyone who worked hard to make this book a reality.

And for the loves of my life, my dogs.

Oh... and also the human loves I'm building a life with, of course. Without them, I would be completely lost.

JENNIFER LEE ROSSMAN

Earlier this year, I was struck by the idea that I needed to edit an anthology, so I filled Jaylee's inbox with questions that basically amounted to "How??????" I didn't expect an invitation to join the *Love & Bubbles* team, but it's been an amazing experience and I'm so grateful for everything I've learned. Thanks Jaylee, for being my first editor, first co-editor, and first friend I made as a grown-up.

Thank you to all of our authors, whose stories still make me smile even after all the times I've read them.

And thank you, everyone in my life who has nodded along and pretended to be interested when I went on and on about slush piles, curly quotation marks, and gay dolphin shapeshifters.

ABOUT THE EDITORS

JAYLEE JAMES is a nonbinary writer, editor, and story curator native to Kansas City who is best known as the editor of *Circuits & Slippers,* an anthology of science-fiction fairytales, and *Vitality Magazine,* which published LGBTQ+ genre fiction between 2014-2016. E also writes a smattering of short fiction and video games. Learn more at JayleeJames.com.

JENNIFER LEE ROSSMAN is a science fiction geek from Oneonta, New York, who has never ever threatened to run over anyone with her wheelchair. Nope, definitely not. Her debut novel, *Jack Jetstark's Intergalactic Freakshow,* will be published in December 2018. She blogs at jenniferleerossman.blogspot.com and tweets @JenLRossman.

Made in the USA
Columbia, SC
12 November 2018